Damnation

Katelyn Taylor

Copyright

Foreword

This is a fictitious depiction of a story inspired by the Salem Witch Trials and what could have occurred. This is in no way historical fact or truth and should be consumed for pleasure. This story is a precursor to the Gallows Hill Trilogy and can be read before or after the trilogy for a better understanding of the fictional history. (No, don't worry, the trilogy is not written in old English)

Trigger Warning

Please proceed with caution! Not only is this book spicy and filled with triggers, it is also a NON HEA. Let that sink in. I know, I know, we love our HEA, but if you've read the Gallows Hill Trilogy then you know, none of the members of the Brethren deserve an HEA. This is written as a foundation for the warped and demented society we all know and loathe. If you are here for a unique take on what could have happened in the Trials (according to this world) and wouldn't mind some nice spice thrown in then sit back, buckle up and enjoy the horrific show.
The following content includes but is not limited to:
Murder, hangings, witchcraft, attempted suicide, death of a child, abuse from a spouse, cheating, graphic torture, explicit sexual scenes, explicit language, non-HEA, and more.

Dedication

To the fuckers that tried to eradicate witches in the Trials, you missed more than one.

Prologue

You may think you know what occurred during the Salem Witch Trials, but let me assure you, this tale is not one you've heard before. In a Puritan village on the East Coast of what would soon become America, a great evil existed, though it might not be the kind you were led to believe.

Though many believe once the Trials were through, that was the end of it, but you and I both know there is more to it than that. After all, the hysteria from the Trials did not end in 1693, it merely evolved.

Over 200 people were accused of witchcraft between 1692 and 1693. Twenty souls perished, and countless were lucky enough to escape a similar fate. Were the history books correct and all those charged truly innocent? Were the people of Salem rightfully overwhelmed with the fear of imminent evil knocking at the door of their village? Or was there a third side?

They always say there are three versions to a story: yours, theirs, and the truth.

What really happened over three hundred years ago will always be left open to interpretation.

Here is mine.

Sit back, relax, and allow yourself to be taken back in time to determine once and for all what really happened in the small village of Salem, Massachusetts.

Chapter One

Thomas

September 12th, 1691

The air is colder now, with autumn fast underway. The harvest has begun, and this season is proving to be a prosperous one indeed. My wife Ann is doing well with managing the household and our seven children, though I can't deny my patience with her wanes by the day. The entitlement and disrespect she serves those around her has everyone confused as to who truly owns a majority of the land in Salem. Thought to be a kind and gentle woman when we first married, disdain is a more appropriate word to describe my affections for my wife these days.

Setting down my pen, I look over my words as the ink settles into the pages of my leatherbound journal. I've been carrying this with me for years now, typically only writing in it from time to time when I'm in need of a cathartic release.

From the outside, I live a charmed life. Being one of the most successful businessmen and landowners in a small village like Salem, Massachusetts definitely has its benefits. So does being well connected with good friends like Samuel Parris, the town's reverend. The only two things that our townsfolk seem to care about are our crops and our God.

Unfortunately, it somehow feels like it's not enough.

My brother, Edward, steps through the door, paying little mind or care to the fact that I do not wish him to be here.

"Brother." He nods. "I'm heading to the tavern, will you join me?"

I sigh, closing my journal and tucking it into the inner pocket of my jacket as I stand.

"Why do you feel the need for company when you're such a proficient consumer all by yourself?"

Edward throws his head back like I am the most amusing man to walk the Earth.

"No truer words have ever been spoken, but do not deny you want an excuse to be away from Ann, Thomas."

I grimace at that and nod, gesturing for him to lead the way.

We walk through my expansive house as we head for the tavern. This house was a painstakingly slow project. We could have very well built something half the size twice as fast, but my father always spoke of proving your wealth, your worth. He recounted through my boyhood that a fine house makes a fine man, and I was determined to be the finest in the village. Arrogant of me? Absolutely, but it's that arrogance that has put me where I am today.

My home is just down the road from the center of the village. It affords me the illusion of privacy while providing the comforts of anything my dependents or I shall desire. People mill about the village, tending to their businesses and homes as Edward and I step through the doors of Ingersoll's Tavern. Nathaniel Ingersoll is behind the bar, nodding to us as he pours Joseph Hutchinson a beer. Edward and I take a seat at our usual table when Nathaniel moves to us.

"What will you be having?" he asks.

"Two whiskeys, Nathaniel. Many thanks." Edward nods at the bar owner.

Nathaniel moves behind the bar just as trouble in human form stumbles in from the back. My brother's love of drink hardly compares to the devotion Thomas Preston holds for it. The man single-handedly keeps Ingersoll's alive and well, I swear it.

"Friends!" he cheers happily, slurring his words as he drops into the empty seat at our table.

I mutter under my breath with displeasure. I've never been too fond of Preston. Never been too fond of many in this village aside from Parris and my brother, really. Preston is not the finest company to keep, but he provides a level of entertainment in an otherwise uneventful town, and after enough libations, he's almost tolerable.

"What has you in such high spirits?" Edward pokes fun.

"God has bestowed the highest glory unto me and my own. Why not have such a spirit about the day?"

"What glory might that be, Preston? The bravery to get out of bed in the morning?" I scoff.

"That as well." He nods, as if I were providing him with another thing to be grateful for.

Dizzy fool.

"My cattle gave life to three calves the morning after last. Rebecca was sure we would lose at least one, but they grow stronger by the day. Imagine! Four cattle of my very own. We shall want no more!"

My brother does him the good service of feigning interest, whereas I shake my head in irritation and focus on the drink Nathaniel hands to me. Some men are so grateful for so little. Do not forsake me for an unholy man, I, too, believe in God's gift of blessings all the same, but thick heads like Preston fail to realize you ought not wait for gifts to be thrust upon you, but rather be persistent in the pursuit of them, and your blessings will grow tenfold. He has not, which is why he is nearly forty-seven years of age and with what to show? I suppose I should rejoice for the poor fool, though, may he embody happiness wherever he may find it.

Round after round is brought to the table until we are all good and subdued.

"How hath I guessed I'd find you heathens here," Parris tuts, though there is no judgment in his tone.

"Come off it, Sam, and have a drink," I say as I relax into my stool and allow my head to lull.

"None for me when I have a sermon tomorrow. I expect you all there, presentable for God and the village."

"All hail God!" Edward shouts before dissolving into a fit of laughter.

Samuel gives my moronic brother a disappointed frown before shaking his head. I gesture for Nathaniel, slipping him more than enough to cover our table's dues before standing to my feet. Preston does the same as Edward tries and fails to do so. Samuel helps me lift him to his feet, one arm over either of our shoulders as we begin walking outside of Ingersoll's.

We don't make it far before my brother is stumbling to the bushes, emptying his gut of all its contents.

"Easy there, Edward," Samuel says, clapping his back as he continues to retch.

My head shakes at the drunk before my eyes pause. I attempt to look away, but it's becoming increasingly harder each time I see her.

Sarah.

Sarah Good is the wife of William Good, a lazy laborer at best. The man spends more time unemployed than at work, leaving his wife to provide for their family and daughter the only way she can;

to beg. The majority of the townsfolk look down upon the Goods, and for good reason. They have nothing to offer or contribute to the village. They are burdens to our society, and yet I've never been able to look away from her.

I'm certain she has no clue the effect she has on me. She no doubt would have exploited it by now if she did, and I'd have willingly allowed it. She has a hold on me unlike anything I've ever experienced.

"Have you laid your eyes upon something valuable, brother?" Edward slurs.

His words cause me to jolt as I abruptly look away from the beggar woman I have no business allowing to occupy my mind.

"No, just averting my eyes from the horror that is my little brother."

He feigns a spear to the heart as he smirks, standing a little taller since his upheaval.

"How you wound me, Thomas."

Shaking my head, I turn to Parris.

"I've got him from here. Until tomorrow," I say.

"God be with you," Samuel says.

"And you both as well," I say to Samuel and Preston before assisting my brother on the walk back to our homes.

Not before stealing one more glance at Sarah, though.

Chapter Two

Sarah

My body aches as I rise for the day. Dorothy stirs in my arms as we sit up. Our bed wasn't safe last night, not after William consumed his first drink. He only delivered a few hits to my face before I took Dorothy into my arms and locked us in the broom closet. Countless hours passed by with William beating on the door before the pounding stopped and we were able to take rest. Unfortunately, our dirt floors hardly bear a comfortable sanctuary, and my body screams in punishment.

"Mama? Is it safe?"

I fight back tears, not allowing a single one to drop as I smile at my sweet girl. She's only five years of age. It isn't fair. This life she was born into isn't fair.

"Yes, my love. God has gifted us another day together, let us take thanks and joy in it."

She smiles at me sleepily, her deep brown hair and green eyes a reflection of my own. Together, we stand as I open the door first, carefully peering out before allowing it to fully open. A few steps and I see William passed out on our bed, snoring heavily. I take relief in moments like these. We ought to be getting ready for church at this time of the day, but with William's state, I'm too afraid to wake him and much too afraid of what will come if Dorothy and I show alone. People will whisper, talk, and William will blame me for all of the sort.

So, I decide to grab the last crust of bread we have, handing it to Dorothy alongside some water I fetched last night before we head into town. I look up in the sky and see that it would not have mattered if I had woken William. Church is well on its way to being over, and soon the town will be streaming with townsfolk, hopefully one more generous than the last.

I hate who I have become. A beggar woman. It's humiliating, disgraceful, but with William's temper and inconsistent work, we're barely surviving as is. We have no other hope. My stomach groans in agony as I try to recount the last day I had a meal. Must be going on three days as of this morning. Every scrap I can manage, I pass to Dorothy, but I feel the weight of my decisions in the sway of my steps.

"Are you okay, Mama?" she asks, her little hand delicately tucked into mine as our feet move down the dirt road.

I conjure the most convincing smile I am able, nodding at my sweet girl.

"Of course. Why don't you ask Mrs. Osborne if you can help her stock the shelves?" I say as I gesture to Sarah Osborne's shop.

Sarah and her husband have some of the most fruitful land in the village, and she truly has a special touch with her jarred spices and crops. Dorothy smiles at me, nodding as she releases my hand and runs inside.

Sarah and I are not quite friends, but more so friendly. Friendlier than any others in this village, I'd say. Neither of us quite fit with the others, and that's okay with us. We believe one day things will change, for we are both gifted in ways others are not. My mother had passed down to me recipes and remedies that heal. From a belly ache to poison, I create various tonics and tinctures that Sarah sells from time to time in her shop, discreetly, of course. The practice of such is not looked upon with fondness, so we both ensure that our business is conducted as privately as possible. The only other member in town who knows of my work is likely Tituba, the Parris's servant. She too practices rituals and remedies from her homeland, though she dabbles too close to the line of darkness for my liking.

I stand off to the side from Sarah's shop, and I see her peek through the doorway, offering me a compassionate greeting before stepping back inside. I nod to her as the church doors swing all the way open, and the townsfolk begin this way into town. My stomach turns unpleasantly as I attempt to swallow my pride and focus on why I'm here. Even if I can walk away with a piece of rye or a pence or two, it shall leave us in a better position than when we rose this morning.

From the moment our eyes meet, Sarah Abbey and Sarah Gadge sneer with disdain, turning their heads to the side. I'll never understand why so many choose to name their children the same. Most people in our small village bear the names Sarah, Thomas, or John. Originality is certainly lacking in our land, there is no doubt of that.

I've never gotten off well with either of them. Both have denied me in my harshest of times, only delivering cruelty and hatred. For such self-proclaimed holy women, you really ought not know it.

Dozens of others pass by, only sparing me an unsatisfied look or grimace, as if I wish to be here, as if I wish to be the pathetic beggar woman with a husband who hates her so. I feel a tear slip down my cheek, refusing the banishment I beg of it before it settles into the corner of my mouth. The cut left from my husband's hand stings, and I look down at my feet in an attempt to conceal the pain and the emotion.

When I lift my head again, my vision is blurry, but I do my best to temper myself when I lock eyes with him.

A man I've known for so long, yet speak with rarely.

One who always lingers but never stays.

A married man with many children.

The same man I often dream about most nights, though I know far better than to.

Thomas Putnam.

He's one of the wealthiest men in the village, the most respected, no doubt. It would tarnish his reputation just to be near me. So, why is he walking towards me with purpose?

My heart beats in my chest heavily, my hands going cold with fright, or maybe excitement. I'm too unwell to tell the difference. His long legs consume the distance between us as many begin casting wary glances towards him. He pays them no mind, though, his deep brown eyes never falling from my own gaze.

When we are just a pace apart, he pauses, nodding his head in greeting.

"Good morrow," he greets.

I attempt to speak, but my words fail me for longer than I'm able to bear. Finally, I collect my voice and return his greeting.

"Good morrow, Mr. Putnam."

"It's Thomas, won't you call me that?" he asks, his eyes never falling from my own for even a moment.

My mouth opens to respond before sound finally leaves it once more.

"Thomas."

I worry that, to his ears, his name from my lips sounds as desired as it feels on mine. It must, because his body tightens and his chest heaves with a heavy breath before he clears his throat.

"I did not see you in church this morning. Are you well?"

I attempt to smile, to assure him I'm fine, but I wince the instant I attempt so. My mouth stings, and it seems to attract his attention.

His eyes focus on it with great detail before a darkness clouds his face. I watch in curiosity as his jaw tightens several times before he speaks.

"Did you and Mr. Good have a disagreement?"

I wish, maybe then I could continue to convince myself that I deserved his anger. Instead, I am merely a casualty of his wrath. For so long, I deluded myself to the idea that he would get better, that the last time would be the last time. I've grown wiser, unfortunately, and such fantastical notions have soon left as my age has grown. It is not out of the ordinary for a husband to "guide" his wife physically, but the manner in which my own does...I wouldn't wish it upon the worst of enemies.

"In so little words," I respond, a sad smile touching my face as I do.

"'Tis the third time this week, is it not?" Thomas asks.

How could he possibly know that? Has he been watching me far closer than I realize? Our lands are quite a distance from one another, and though our paths cross from time to time, this is the first conversation we have ever shared.

I do not speak. I know better than to do so, especially when I have nothing but disparaging remarks when it comes to my husband. Thomas nods like he already knows my answer for himself before reaching into his pocket and pulling out five pence. My eyes widen as he holds it out for me. When I do not offer my hand, impatience fills his features as he takes my hand with his free one, dropping the silver coins into my hand before closing it with his.

Flutters fill my stomach, and my heart begins beating thunderously once more as his hold on my hand remains.

"Tell him you collected one, then keep the rest for yourself. Do you understand me?"

I shake my head, rendered speechless.

"I-I cannot. I cannot accept so much from you. I do not require so much—"

"You do, Mrs. Good. You deserve…far more."

His words suspend in the air between us, causing me to feel faint as I look up to him.

"Sarah."

He rolls his lips together like he is reconsidering whether to speak so informally. Being the impulsive man I have seen him to be, though, he does not waste another moment.

"Sarah, please. I insist upon it."

You would think I am daft the way I have found myself unable to form any considerable amount of words in this man's presence. Perhaps I am, though, because I cannot understand why a man with a reputation such as his, one known for his greediness and narcissism, would be so generous. Especially generous to an unfortunate woman such as myself.

"Thank you…Thomas," I say, pausing for a moment before using his name.

If there is a single listener into the conversation, the scandal would very well ravage the village before nightfall. My eyes scan our surroundings, relieved to find us alone. Who would believe a gossiper as it is? They would think the person had gone mad. Thomas Putnam and…myself? Outlandish.

"Thomas!" his brother Edward calls out, his strides carrying him towards us faster than I'd care.

In an instant, Thomas drops his hold on my hands, forcing a chill to consume my body, and turns away to face his brother. I know the gesture is meant to be dismissive, but why do I feel more so protected, as if he was shielding me from his brother, from the rest of the village? It must be my own delusions once more.

"Brother, Ann is looking for you." I hear Edward say.

Peering around Thomas, I find Edward staring at me with deep curiosity before his eyes return to his brother.

"Should I tell her you are otherwise engaged?"

There is a teasing tone that I'm not certain I enjoy before Thomas speaks.

"Of course not, on my way then."

I think that is it, until Thomas turns to face me once more, nodding his head as he speaks.

"God be with you, Mrs. Good."

"God be with you, Mr. Putnam," I say. "And you as well, Mr. Putnam."

Edwards casts an uneasy glance to me before reaching into his pocket and flicking a pence. It hits my chest before falling to the ground. I fight the urge to pick it up, not interested in the disrespectful show he is no doubt attempting to orchestrate.

"Well manners are rewarded with well pay, Mrs. Good. My sincerest hope you do not forget that. It may be the very thing to save that agreeable face from similar treatment, yes?" He smirks, gesturing at my cut lip.

An angered noise escapes Thomas before he grips Edward's arm, ripping him away from me and storming down the road towards their homes. I cannot clearly hear the impassioned words they speak to one another, and I truly am grateful for that. The disrespect of the village, while should be tiresome, never fades. The pain never stops, and each disparaging look and comment pricks at myself on the inside like no strike ever could.

Once they are out of sight, I quickly bend down, grabbing the pence that Edward flicked at me. My pride begged me not to, but my mind was victorious over that battle.

Six pence. That's more than William has ever made in a week, let alone a day.

Tis more than I have ever held in my hand at one time. I find myself quickly concealing the coins, stepping into Sarah's shop to purchase as much food as I can manage for a pence while keeping the other five hidden, just as Thomas instructed.

Chapter Three

Thomas

"Where has thou been?" Ann interrogates the moment I step foot onto our land.

Irritation rises inside me as I move past her without a word.

"Has thou become hard of hearing, or simply too daft to understand the words I speak?" she sneers.

"Silence!" I command. "You hold no right for my agenda, nor the time spent achieving it. Though you often forget, I am your husband, you are my wife, and you will be *silent*!"

I am a better man than my father was, I have always tried to be, at the very least. My father would often speak to my mother like so. Watching as a young boy, I saw how it hurt her, and I vowed to treat my own wife better when the time came. If I had known I'd have married so painfully, I might not have made such insurmountable promises.

Moving through my home, several of my children are spread around in the main room. Ann is pulling on Elizabeth's hair before shoving her to the ground. Sisters fight just as brothers do, but those two are the most nuisance of our bunch. Pair Ann and Parris's daughter together, and 'tis a frightful time indeed. My wife has much to teach that girl before she is ready for marriage, which is a feat I am unsure she will achieve on account of the likeness she shares with her mother. Had my father not struck a deal with Ann's involving a small fortune, I would not be in this position. Ann's father knew what an ache his daughter was, just as I know my own. You will not see me wasting away money to marry her off, though. She must learn to be better.

Stepping through the doorway of my bedroom, I pause for a moment before reaching for the whiskey jar. I rarely take to drink in my home, but an exception must be made for this moment. Opening the top, I take three large mouthfuls before resting it on the table. The harsh sting is accompanied by a soothing warmth that tempers...everything. My irritation, my exhaustion...my desire.

Pulling out my journal from my coat pocket, I flip open the black leather book, reaching for a feather and ink as I begin.

I saw her again this day. Instead of averting my gaze as I often do, I held it. I held it for so long that my feet carried me to her, as if I were not of my own control. As if God himself had thrust me towards her. As I shared the very air she had just exhaled, I reveled in being so near to her.

My heart was pounding so loud I could hear it in my own ears. My eyes roamed over her from top to bottom, from her well worn blue and white dress to her bare feet. She has close to nothing, yet she embodies...everything. She is warmth and kindness; she is perseverance and strength. She is light...a light I hath found myself drawing dangerously close to with little to no moral confliction. What has thou done to me? As if she had commanded I am hers and, just so, I have no qualms or opposition.

God, forgive me for the sinful thoughts that ravage my mind when I am near her. Forgoing all that I know about her situation as well as my own, I want her. In every way God has created possible, I desire her more deeply than a man starved desires nourishment.

Taking a breath for a moment, I shake my head. I must banish these sinful notions. I am, after all, a Puritan man first and foremost. A man of God, and a married one at that. Just as she too is married. No woman is worth an eternity swimming in rivers of hellfire. Though, dare I be so bold to think that Sarah Good very well falls close. The closest this land has ever seen, I have no doubt of it.

From her shining green eyes to her skin as smooth as milk, she is perfectly made in God's image, and I cannot stop the way I yearn for her. The way I always have. The moment my skin touched hers, though, I knew my strength would be tested. My morals. My faith. Sarah Good will no doubt be my greatest rise and my sharpest of falls. If I allowed her so.

I cannot allow this of her.

I oversee my staff as they harvest this year's crops when a figure catches my attention yonder. My feet are moving before I command them to do so, carrying me closer to the road and further from my responsibilities. I ought not know how my gut knew it was her before my eyes could so plainly see. Somehow, I just knew, and now Sarah Good is a short stone's throw away, walking from door to door, though she misses my own as well as my brother's.

I watch as she approaches the Abbey home. My ears do not catch their conversation, but I can hear well enough the argument they are having before Jonathan Abbey slams the door inches from her face.

Sarah turns away, muttering something beneath her breath as I cross the road, inserting myself into her path. She startles for a moment as her eyes come to me.

"Mr. Putnam. My apologies, I did not see you."

"You need not apologize for the path I have chosen to walk, though I will accept one in honor of your excessive formality," I say, giving her a barely there grin to show my playful intent.

She accepts it with a smile of her own as she nods.

"Thomas," she whispers, so sweetly 'tis like sugar to my ears, no matter the ridiculousness of that thought.

"What adventures does this day bring to you?" I ask.

Her smile slips away as a far off look takes over her face.

"The same one I walk each day, I suppose."

The air between us hangs heavily for several moments before she looks back to me once more.

"And you?"

I slip my hands into my pocket, not attempting to hide the golden pocket watch tucked inside my coat. Her eyes move to it, transfixed by the glinting metal in the shining sun. I am not a modest man, and I have never attempted to convey such. I am proud of what I have earned, of what I have built, and I do not hate the position and favor it gains me from others in return.

"The usual duties. Overseeing this year's harvest, preparing for sale and shipment to Boston."

"A farmer's life is nary dull," she says with that smile I have grown to adore returning once again.

"Especially when it sprawls across the distance my own does," I boast.

Am I being too arrogant? Perhaps. Something in me seeks her

approval desperately, though. As if a beggar woman's opinion matters at all. It does, though. Hers does, to me.

"You are a blessed man indeed." She nods in agreement.

"Not in all the ways that count," I say, unable to stop myself as the truth of my life spills from my lips.

Sarah tilts her head in curiosity when a voice calls out down the road.

"Sarah! Damned woman! Get your arse over here now!"

We both turn to see William Good approaching with haste, fury rolling off him in waves as he closes the distance. I take note of the fear that fills her body as she sees him, tensing as his hand reaches out, yanking her closer to his side.

Without considering the consequences, I take a step towards her, as if I were ready to free her from his grasp at a moment's notice. William looks to me with a sneer, despite knowing better.

"Putnam, I did not notice thee."

"Good," I greet stiffly, not offering a single nicety to a man who deserves no such thing.

When he understands he will not be receiving any further greeting, he turns to his wife, increasing his hold onto her.

"Come, I have no patience to chase you all over the village."

"I was trying to collect, as you commanded," she says, snapping back far more than I'd expect for a woman in her position.

Irritation flickers upon his face as he raises his hand as if to strike her before he thinks better of it, casting his gaze to me. Well. The savage knows how to behave in good society when forced to.

"I am sure you have made not a single pence. You waste your time with looks as such," he says, gesturing to her.

Perhaps if he would not mar her face with welts and bruises, she would be able to look more favorably.

He begins to drag her away as I call out to them.

"Good."

They both turn, tears beginning to build in Sarah's eyes as I step forward, reaching into my pocket and holding out two pence. William's eyes widen with surprise as Sarah gently holds her hand out for me.

"God be with you," I say, speaking only to her.

"God be with you," she repeats, nodding with the sentiment.

In a moment, William snatches the coins from her grasp, pocketing them as he continues dragging her down the road. I watch them walk until they disappear beyond the horizon.

———

It be the next nightfall when I take to a walk to the creek. My property holds most of the land to gain access to the creek, so it is all but my own. There are small alcoves you can slip through from the other side of town, but most take to other means for their water.

Ann is putting the children to bed after yet again raising her temper with me over her allowance of all things. The woman is the richest in all of Salem, yet she still takes ire with me. I could not speak, so irate with her that I stood from the table and made my way to the cool, brisk air, gaining much needed relief.

To my understanding, a fabric merchant from Boston had come through town, attempting to sell his finest silks. The cost was too much for even Ann to afford on her allowance, and therefore, she blames me for her embarrassment.

I cannot help but scoff at the notion. That woman has never known struggle, known suffering. I hand her a shilling and 'tis not enough, but I hand Sarah Good five pence as I did the other morning and...she looked as if she were on the verge of tears. As if all her life would somehow come together. Do not mistake me, five pence is the equivalent of what Ann receives in two weeks' time.

Regardless, I had never witnessed gratitude like hers before. It took every bit of strength inside me not to reach into my pocket once more and offer her everything I had. Whatever I possessed, I desired her to have it more, which was quite a strange feeling. Though I'd never speak it aloud, to be granted the permission to hold her hands in my own for a little longer, I would have walked away from her a penniless man in exchange.

Then my arse of a brother came along, spoiling the moment and my mood. And then the following moment stolen with her, William came along and spoilt that as well.

The disrespect he showed her had my fists clenching, readying themselves to cease his actions and words. As Sarah does, she remained silent and steadfast, no matter the whispers or glares she receives. She remained unmoving and still. No matter how deeply I yearn to gather her into my arms and shield her from any ill notions or words, she did not need me. Perhaps that is why I desire her so.

As my feet carry me to the creek, I hesitate when I see a figure on the other side. My hand moves to the pistol on my hip, first thoughts conjuring a bear or wild cat. They have been known to wander this area, especially before winter's arrival.

Upon a closer look, my hand moves away from the pistol. Not a wild cat or bear, but human.

A soft sound echoes through the creekside, drawing me nearer. I cannot understand the words, or maybe it's because there aren't any. All I hear is a woman's voice humming a tune as she bathes in the creek beneath the moonlight.

The sound is mesmerizing as I take step after step towards the carrier of such melody. My feet only cease once I have reached the creek bed, and the woman before me becomes clear.

Sarah.

She is dressed in only her undergarments, the white slip dress clinging to her skin as she pours a bucket upon herself. The water soaks her clothing, forcing it to become more transparent. I feel myself hardening at the sight of her, and though I know how wrong it is just to be looking upon her, God himself would have to pluck my eyesight to force me to do so.

Sarah continues humming that familiar tune, swaying beneath the moonlight as she turns and faces me. Her nipples are hard, poking through the thin material as it clings to every curve of hers. My eyes roam up and down over her before her eyes meet my own.

Horror flashes in them as she lets out a screech. She begins to run through the creek for the grass, and before I can resist my urges, I'm chasing her like a hunter to his prey.

My feet pound against the rocky bed of the creek as water reaches my knees. That does nothing to deter my hunt. Sarah's dress offers her great resistance in her escape, and I thank God for it because I catch her all that easier.

When my hand goes to her mouth to cease her screams, we tumble to the ground, her back landing against the grass while our feet are still in the water.

"Hush, hush, 'tis me. It's Thomas," I assure her.

Sarah's eyes are wide with fear, but upon hearing my name, her screaming ceases, and her fear vanishes. Something inside of me enjoys the peace my presence seems to bring her. I enjoy that far too much, actually.

Slowly, I remove my hand from her mouth, resting it on the other side of her head in the grass, suspending the upper half of my body above hers while our legs are still tangled together in the river.

"T-thomas?" she questions breathily. "What are you doing here?"

I tilt my head to the side curiously, my tone attempting to sound chastising, though the smile that spreads across my face betrays me.

"What am I doing near *my* creek? What are you doing, Mrs. Good, bathing in the moonlight on my property?"

"I was not," she rushes on to say, shaking her head quickly. "I stayed on this side. I made sure of it. I...I always bathe here at night."

That captures my attention. The common creek is far closer to her home. To get here is a great walk, especially wet after bathing.

"Why?" I question.

Her full lips part, but they don't say a word. I feel my heart beating in my chest so loudly, I wonder if she too can feel it, or at the very least, hear it. I'm unsure if it is the silence the night brings, the privacy, or the fact of being in this woman's presence turns me into a man I do not recognize, but the words spill from my lips despite better judgment.

"I rather enjoy the idea of you bathing in my creek."

Sarah's eyebrows come together curiously.

"Y-you do?"

My head moves up and down, my eyes never leaving hers.

"Very much."

A choppy exhale escapes her as her own eyes roam my face, so many thoughts running through her mind, I'd give anything just to pluck one and hear it for myself.

"I have to go, Mr. Putnam. If someone were to see us in this way—"

"Thomas," I insist.

A soft look passes upon her face as she nods.

"Thomas. You're...you're on top of me."

I blink, as if the very idea of how this would look to others had just now crossed my own mind. In this moment, I feel her everywhere. I feel her legs resting on either side of my own. I feel my thigh pressed against her center, the warmth of it forcing my length to twitch in desire. She must be able to feel me because her body stills at the feeling.

My eyes slowly move from where we are tangled to her own.

"Apologies, Mrs. Good."

"Sarah," she says, just above a whisper, her chest heaving as she does.

My gaze moves down to see her left breast desperate to escape the confines of her dress. I watch her hardened nipple strain against the wet fabric to the point my own mouth waters with desire, craving nothing more than taking her into my mouth.

An action I never could have imagined in all my forty years on this world, Sarah's hand slowly lifts, shaky fingers grasping the top of her fabric, dragging it down to expose her breast.

"Does this please you, Thomas?"

A growl akin to an animal rolls through my chest as my eyes greedily take in the sight before me. I'm struggling in this moment. Every bit of decorum and strength I have is being tested as I look upon this perfect woman, offering herself to me as if she were the meal I've long craved.

"I am a man of God," I say through clenched teeth.

"And I, a woman of God," she agrees.

"This is wrong. 'Tis adultery," I say as my hand comes down, skating across the silky, smooth skin of her breast.

Her back arches, a breathy sigh escaping her as she nods.

"'Tis indeed."

My hand cups her full breast, holding it into my hand as I lower my mouth to her. I feel the good, holy man I know myself to be leaving my body as a sinner of moral depravity takes over. And my apologies to you, God, I welcome him.

"Tell me to stop, Sarah. Tell me that you do not want me. Tell me you never wish to lay eyes on me again, nor have my touch upon your skin," I practically beg.

She looks down at me before I feel her hand cup the back of my head. Her fingers lightly run through my hair, and for a moment, I close my eyes at the comfort it brings me. When I open my eyes again, Sarah is watching me with a look that is akin to the feeling inside me.

Fear, desperation, desire.

"I cannot lie to you, Thomas."

That is it. That is all it takes to transform me from a good, holy man of God to a sinner bound for hell.

My mouth wraps around her nipple, tongue swirling around the stiff peak as she gasps with pleasure, rubbing her center against me with desperate need. I afford her breasts all the attention I can possibly give, and then some, before my hands move to her dress, lifting it up to her hips and exposing her naked body. It is perfection.

I am fumbling with my belt buckle, peeling off my clothes as fast as I can manage before I am lining myself to her. Sarah's legs fall open, welcoming me inside her, but I don't push. Instead, I stay there a moment, dragging the tip of myself through her. She is so wet and so warm, practically luring me inside. I have laid my lips upon her skin, for that is true, but this, this is the moment that will be unforgivable, detestable. I feel my morality shaking as I grapple with what to do next.

"Once we do this…there is no going back, Sarah," I say, my voice straining.

Conflict rises on her face as she frowns.

"Should we not?"

I could scream. Do not do this to me. Do not make me the decider. I would have given anything for her to push down on me, taking away my hand and absolving me of guilt, truly, because I already know I have no choice in this matter.

Keeping myself lined up to her without pushing in, I rest my nose against hers, cupping her face tenderly.

"No, we should not."

My lips press to hers in the same moment I push inside her. Sarah whimpers as I ease myself inside her, inch by inch. Her tongue swirls against my own, forcing me to pull out of her before thrusting back in harder this time. In a moment that will no doubt be my most ashamed to face on judgement day, I've never felt so good in all my life.

She holds me tight, clenching me in a way that has me ready to finish in an instant. I want this to last, though. I pull away from her lips, though I don't last long before stealing another kiss and another. Addiction. Far greater than any tobacco or drink anyone could ever offer. Sarah Good is human embodied addiction. I'm sure of it now that God put her on this earth just to tempt me, and I'm ashamed to say, temptation won. I'm not sorry, though.

"Thomas," she moans. "I never dreamt this moment would come."

"Nor I, my love," I say through clenched teeth, making a point to hold her face gently as I thrust in and out of her.

"My love?" she whispers.

"What else could this draw be? You were created for me, Sarah Good. Whether to bless me or torment me, perhaps both. 'Tis not the point nor the matter. You. Are. My. Own."

With each thrust, she moves against me more, and I feel the creeping in of my own release. Her legs wrap around my back, locking me into place, and I groan as I feel myself begin to pulse. I know I should discover how far into her cycle she is. I should at the very least pull out of her before finishing. Something in that notion feels incredibly wrong, though, and instead, I push inside her deeper, allowing my release to wash over me.

I moan into her shoulder, continuing my thrusts as her own release finds her. Our shouts of pleasure are drowned out by the running creek beside us, only the midnight sky a witness to what we have just done.

When the euphoria from our pleasure fades and our breathing settles, I look down at her, expecting to find regret. To my surprise, I find a smile. Dare I say the most beautiful smile to ever be gifted.

I do not speak, particularly because there is nothing to say. We both know this was wrong. We are both married, with children, no less. Both people of God who have just come together as man and wife outside of marriage. We have not only committed a sin, we have become sin. Especially due to the fact that this will not be the last time. I will not allow it.

Chapter Four

Sarah

As I finish tying my bonnet around my head, my fingers trail down my neck, resting on the sensitive skin that Thomas touched. It has been six nights since we... I can't even bear to think it in my own head. I'm completely unsure of what came over me, of what came over us both. More so, I have been praying and begging God to help me each day since, because where I should feel guilt and disgust, I feel...joy, excitement, desire. Not only am I not ashamed, I want it again, him again. I want...more.

Pushing those sinful thoughts away, I intend to clear my head before my family and I head to this morning's service at the church. William did not take to drink last night, I assume due to the fact he has run out of our money. Dorothy and I would be long starved if it wasn't for what Thomas had given us last week. I'll accept William's purchases as a blessing, though, because when the bottle is dry and long gone, he is my William once more. Not a loving man, nor a kind one, but he is not a harmful one either, and for that, I am grateful.

"Make haste, Sarah. We shall need to leave immediately," he says as he steps into the room.

I nod in obedience as I look down at our daughter. Dorothy is dressed as neatly as I was able, her hair perfectly tucked beneath her bonnet as she smiles up at me.

"We are ready," I say, holding my hand out for Dorothy's as she slips it into my own.

William nods, straightening his black hair and coat before leading us through the door. The sun is bright this morning, giving promises to a new day. If I am correct, 'tis also a new moon tonight. The moon has such wonderful properties to be harnessed on a day such as this. My tonics and aides are often amplified beneath a full moon's collection. Once William has gone to sleep, I'll slip out of the house to do my gatherings and bring Sarah Osborne my items in the morning. Depending on her mood, I may even earn enough to buy Dorothy a new dress or shoes.

The walk to the town's church is not long at all, and soon enough, we are stepping inside the wooden building, taking a seat in a pew towards the back. The front of the church is reserved for those who deem themselves the holiest and purest of the town. Surely, a beggar woman and her drunkard of a husband would never earn such a title.

Reverend Parris is at the front, encouraging his daughter Betty and niece Abigail to take a seat. Several prying eyes meet my own, displeasure at our attendance abundantly clear on their faces. I pay them no mind, though, as I focus my eyes forward and listen with intention.

"Brothers, sisters, what a blessed day to live in God's glory," the reverend booms. "Let us take prayer in the blessing of us coming together."

We all close our eyes, bowing our heads as he leads us in prayer.

"God, we thank thee for thy gifts you have displayed upon us this week. Crops and cattle are in abundance from your blessings. Ailments are being healed, and lives are being created, all to you.

We ask that you guide us through your will this next week, as we open our hearts and minds to follow you more diligently, feverishly, and wholly. Amen."

"Amen," the congregation agrees as we all look up once more.

When I do, my eyes blink open to land on one face in particular.

Thomas.

He's turned into his seat, his eyes on me. 'Tis not for long, and his expression lacks much depth. His eyes, though. They sear into my skin, as if they could see into my very soul. The softest smile touches his mouth in a secretive way that sends a fluttering feeling rushing through me.

In the next moment, he is turning around, his wife Ann looking around the room as if to find what holds her husband's interest so. It takes everything in me not to meet her eyes, as I feign interest in Reverend Parris's sermon.

The reverend goes on for a long while about being pure for God. Following his will and order and the consequences that fall if you shall not. I must say, the timing of the sermon feels quite coincidental. Then again, that could be the rising guilt inside me speaking.

Once the sermon is over, everyone begins filing out of the church, making their way on for the day. Near the doors, things get quite crowded, and soon, bodies are jostled and bumping into one another. I try to navigate through, keeping Dorothy close, when a hand grabs mine. I look around and meet Thomas's eyes as he pushes what feels like a piece of parchment into my hand.

I frown in confusion before he forces my hand to close around the parchment, his touch sending goosebumps to race against my skin before he's slipping back into the crowd. My heart beat is racing as I discreetly attempt to tuck the parchment into the waist of my skirt. My eyes are begging to afford me the knowledge of what he has written, but my mind knows better than to risk it here.

William is three paces ahead of us, but all it would take is one look back.

Impatiently, I wait until we are home, excusing myself to the outhouse before shutting the door behind me. Once I do, I hastily pull the parchment out, relieved that it is still there, his script beautifully marking the small page.

Meet me by the creek when the moon is at the peak.

Tonight? I have so much to do beneath the full moon. Perhaps if I start soon enough, I will be finished in time. Am I really doing this? Are we? We are planning an unchaperoned meeting yet again. The last time was an accident, a mistake, you may say. This...this is filled with intention and promise as to what will come.

And I can hardly wait.

I slipped a tonic into William's water. It was a mild sleeping tonic, one he will awake in the morning, drowsy, but well. Nevertheless, I'm a vile woman who is more and more hell bound by the moment. I had no choice, though. Without drink, he cannot sleep, and I needed him to. I have work to do and I have...Thomas. From the moment I read those words on the parchment, I felt as if I could not catch my breath. Not yet again until I saw him.

With one more glance to assure myself Dorothy was sound asleep, accompanied by a snoring William, I made my way out to the creek. I brought along some tonic that I created earlier, as well as some stones I reserve for special times such as these. Once bathed in the moonlight, I begin the practices my mother taught me, cleansing the stones and blessing the tonics with the gift of moonlight. So many would see me at the end of a rope for such things. The small minds of the townsfolk cannot separate the idea of evil influence from the Devil himself and harnessing the gifts and power God has granted the sun, moon, and earth. What I do is only evil if I hold evil intent. I have never, and would never, do such things, but I know better than to allow anyone the knowledge of my practices.

My hands are wrapped around a stone as I finish cleansing it when a snap comes from the distance. My eyes fly open in alert as I peer around in the darkness until a familiar figure steps beneath the moonlight. Quickly, I drop the stone beside my tonics in the basket I brought before covering them with my bonnet.

I reside on one side of the creek while Thomas is on the other. He pauses for a moment at the edge, a smile carving his face that sends that familiar fluttering feeling inside of me before he starts towards me. Long, purposeful steps carry him through the rushing water of the creek, his boots sloshing through until he makes his arrival on my side.

I expect him to greet me, to ask of my day and night, or something of the sort. I did not expect him to close the distance between us, not a sound nor a word escaping him before his lips are on my own.

The air is stolen from my lungs in an instant as I feel my heartbeat in my chest with a fierceness like nothing else. His large hands brace my face tenderly, as if I am the greatest treasure he has ever experienced. When he pulls away, his breath is ragged and rough as his low voice calls to me.

"Good evening, my love."

I cannot stop the smile that adorns my face at the name he has chosen for me. This is absolute madness. No care to the months, years, if I'm honest, that I've watched him, this is all moving so quickly. Too quickly. At least my mind tells me so, my body assures me that I have always been Thomas's. That I was always meant to be.

"Good evening." I smile.

"I missed thee...so," he speaks, shaking his head as if the distance pained him.

"As did I."

He leans in once more, his lips moving against my own before his arms come beneath my legs, lifting me into the air. I squirm at the suddenness before he is walking with me in his arms, leading us to a tree. The strength of his arms has me in awe as he presses my back against the tree, lifting the skirt of my dress up before pushing my undergarments down and forcing himself inside me. A plea-sured moan escapes me as he groans.

"Right where I belong," he says as he begins thrusting in and out of me.

Pleasure sparks inside me with each touch, our mouths still pressed to one another as he continues. This sinful act would be so much more abhorrent if it didn't feel so decadent. My legs inter-twine around his back, pushing him deeper inside me.

"Sarah," he moans. "I ache for you, more than anything in this world. You are my greatest desire. 'Tis unfathomable to have you in my arms like so. I've thought about nothing but for so long."

I nod my agreement as another moan escapes me.

"As have I, for months."

He pauses for a moment, his eyes burrowing into my own.

"Longer, my love. So much longer."

My stomach flips at that as he continues thrusting into me. To know he has desired me for as long as I have him, for longer, it secures something inside of me. It gives way to a justification of sorts, though I'm sure there is not a soul alive who would see it the way we do. 'Tis okay, though. The only person's approval I require is Thomas's.

"Finish with me, my love. I want to feel you finish around me," Thomas practically begs.

There is something so meaningful about a powerful man like Thomas begging for someone like me. As I look into his eyes, a warmth spreads inside me. Something more than just lust or desire. Something far too powerful to come to fruition as quickly as it has. But it has, and 'tis glorious.

Pleasure rolls through my body from the tips of my toes to the top of my head. My body shakes in his arms as I lose all control of myself, only existing in a space made up of pleasure and joy. Thomas follows along, jerking inside me as the warmth of his release fills me. What a terrible mistake we have just made. My cycle is linked to the moon in perfect harmony. The dangers of what could come of this moment are high, and I can't help but pray God doesn't allow that to happen, as if he would lift a finger for a sinner like me.

Chapter Five

Sarah

It has been seven Sundays since Thomas and I have begun our affair. We have not spoken of what it means, or what shall come. Instead, we find peace within each other, absorbing the moments we are gifted alone, a break from our reality. His hate for his wife is akin to my disgust of my husband. Yet we both know there could never be a future for us. Not here, not in Salem. 'Tis okay, though, I will take the stolen moments with him with great joy, for they push me forward even on the hardest of days.

As I rise this morning, an ache settles in my breasts, and a wave of sickness plagues my stomach. I do not have to test my theory to know that it is fact. I also know that we did little to nothing to prevent such a thing, so it shouldn't come as a shock. My ignorance wished we would be so lucky. That it shall not take, for William and I tried for so long before being gifted Dorothy. 'Tis been near impossible to have another. I thought perhaps it could be that I was now barren. I now know that to be false. I am with child, and I'm certain with everything in me that the baby growing inside me is not my husband's.

The consequences of my situation rest heavily on my chest.

William and I have laid together several times since Thomas and I began our affair. 'Tis my wifely duty, and though I hate every moment of it, I know I have no choice. However, I also know to be true that it cannot be William's, for I did not lay with him during my fertile window. Only Thomas.

Swallowing roughly, I strain to push down the wave of sickness plaguing me as I struggle to stand. My efforts are a waste as I feel the contents of my stomach begin to rise. Rushing outside, I hardly make it before I am retching up yesterday's supper. Several more times pass before William's voice echoes behind me.

"Are thou sick?"

My hands are shaky as I attempt to wipe the mess from my face, looking over my shoulder at him. Once a handsome man, the drink has made him ugly, accentuating his large nose and blotchy face. The depth of his leathered skin knows no bounds, and there is almost no color left to his hair.

"Yes, I am with child."

He frowns like the news disappoints him, but that does not matter to me. Instead, I await his response with bated breath to see if he questions the child's origin.

"We have barely enough money now. How does thee suggest we provide for another mouth to feed?"

Of course he does not expect there to be another father. I have been a dutiful wife to him. Why would he expect that has changed?

"We will manage," I say with a shaky head.

An evil laugh escapes him before anger consumes his face.

"Thou thinks it be that easy? We will manage? Manage with what money? With what labor? You provide nothing but tonics that do not sell nor work, and Dorothy is too dull to conduct even a simple task!"

"She is a child," I defend.

My tonics do sell and work fantastically so. I just do not let William onto that fact.

"She is useless! What shall I do if you curse me with another girl? No dowry shall ever leave this family. The only good any of ye bring is selling your skin at the pub."

My stomach turns at the thought of William forcing me or our child to do such a heinous thing.

"You're despicable," I spew, only realizing too late that I let it slip.

The next thing I see is William's fist. It comes straight for my eye, sending stars scattering across my mind. Again and again, his fists rain down on me. All I can think to do is curl up tightly, protecting my stomach as best as I'm able, as he releases his fury. My screams of pain echo through the countryside before I feel one last kick to my back.

"Away with you! Go! Collect us a sum, or so help me, the child will be next!"

A choked sob escapes me as his heavy boots stomp away, heading for his work down the road. I'm unsure of how long I lay there. I know there is blood, I can smell it, taste it, but I'm unable to move.

When I hear the small footsteps of Dorothy, 'tis the only thing to force my body to rise.

"Mama?" she calls out.

"Out here, my love. I'm heading to town. You will stay here," I say, keeping my back to her as I face forward.

"I do not wish to be alone. Please let me come."

"No!" I snap hastily as I hear her attempt to face me.

She has seen enough of her father's ugliness, I won't allow her to see me like this if I am able.

"Stay, sweet girl. I shall return soon, with sweets."

"Really? A sweet of my very own?"

"Yes," I promise, knowing full well I will struggle to keep said promise.

"Be safe, Mama!" she calls out as I limp from our home towards town.

I must make it to Sarah Osborne's. She owes me a month's sum. If I hand it to William carefully, he will feel more secure as my pregnancy progresses. And perhaps more village folk will look kindly on me. When I was pregnant with Dorothy, I received much more than ever before from others.

The simple walk to Sarah's shop feels as if it's a march to the gallows, though. My body screams in pain, and my vision blurs as fresh blood drips into my eye. I do my best to keep the space clear before I approach the storefront. With winter coming, goods are more sacred than ever. All townsfolk will be storing for the harsh Salem winter, which means greater sales for Sarah and I both.

"Good day," Sarah greets when she looks upon me. "Or not."

A disappointing chuckle escapes me at her lack of empathy. As I said once before, we are not friends in the slightest.

"What does thou need for this day?" she asks in a tone that tells me she wants nothing more than to be rid of me.

"My wages," I say hollowly.

"Wages?" Sarah asks.

"Yes. For the...products I supply."

"I know nothing of what you speak of. Everything in my shop is grown and cultivated by myself."

Outrage wars inside me as I stare at her, aghast.

"What lies do you speak? You know not that to be the truth!"

"Perhaps, you are welcome to prove otherwise to the sheriff."

My mouth is agape, anguish and anger raging inside me. An evil smile curves her face as she flicks her hand at me.

"Away with you, your unsightly self shall only frighten my dear customers."

"You shall not commit such acts without punishment!" I snap.

She looks taken aback for a moment before closing the distance between us. Her head cocks to the side in a way of intimidation, but the anger inside me does not allow me to feel anything besides such.

"Is thou threatening me? Perhaps I shall fetch the sheriff myself. See what says he in the matter of the living situations you keep for your child out there. She deserves far better. Shall we see what he thinks of this matter entirely?"

Fear and panic stab through me at her words. She sneers at me before shooing me away like a pest. Crippling anger continues to plague me from the inside out as I find myself numbly stepping out of the shop. My only income is gone. It's back to begging if I want to protect myself, my daughter...and the child I now carry, all thanks to that wench. If I were to ever wish death upon one, it would be her. For anyone with such a black heart ought not deserve the gift of a new day.

The air is cold today, which means not many will brave town if not necessary. One by one, I knock on each townsfolk's door, begging, pleading. Few spare me a glance, even fewer spare me a pence. I pause outside Thomas's home before I continue on. There are not enough shillings in the world that would allow me to come face to face with the man I love. Not like this. Not while his child grows inside me, yet the fate of our empty bellies grows with each moment. Unfortunately for me, Ann Putnam sees me as she plays in the yard and yells to her mother.

"Mama! Come quick! The old beggar hag is here!"

Vile little girl.

I make haste in the other direction, attempting to be gone as fast as I am able. Due to the damage left behind from William, it is not fast enough, and I hear Ann's shrewd voice next.

"Away thou foul beggar! I will take personal joy in shooting thee! Trespassing is a crime!"

My head turns to see Ann pointing a gun towards me. Fear

rises inside as she takes aim before Thomas comes running from the house. They grapple with the gun for several moments before it goes off in the sky. Finally, Thomas is able to rip the gun from her hold before fisting the material of her dress as he screams so loud, his lungs will surely be raw.

"Are you mad? You dare commit murder with my weapon? On my property?"

"She's a trespassing beggar! Hardly a soul to miss!" Ann defends.

Fury contorts Thomas's face as he shoves her away. She stumbles for a moment before landing on her back.

"Away with thou fore I lose my temper and do something I ought to!"

Fear staunches her and their child's face as they both run inside. I take the opportunity to continue to flee while Thomas attempts to chase me down.

"Sarah!" he calls out. "Sarah, stop! I command thee!"

For a reason unbeknownst to me, I do as he says, keeping my back to him when I'm far enough down the road. When he approaches, he grips my arm, leading me away from prying eyes. Turning me to face him in the shadows behind the trees, he inhales a sharp breath at the sight of my injuries, his eyes wide with horror.

"What happened to you?"

"William," I say, keeping my eyes low where they belong.

"Why?" he asks, his tone taking on a sharp tint to it.

"Because I spoke out of turn, because we have no money, because I am with child and have greatened that burden," I say, my voice wavering as tears spill down my face.

All the anger is gone from his face, shock being the only remaining emotion.

"You're with child," he repeats.

"Indeed." I nod as another tear falls.

"And it's... William's?" he asks carefully.

My eyes lift to his as silence descends around us.

"You ought know 'tis not the truth."

"Mine?" he asks, his voice cracking softly as if the shock is bleeding into his words.

"Twas dull to think it would not occur," I say as I turn away from him.

"We're having a baby? Together?"

My head whips around to face him, surprise at the lightened tone his words carry.

"You seem far too delighted by such news."

"How can I be anything else? My love carries my child." He smiles. A great smile that he only gifts me at our creekside.

His hand tenderly cups my cheek, taking care not to touch anywhere injured as he speaks.

"God has never blessed me with a greater gift than to give me a life with you."

My heart soars, but my mind argues.

"What life do you speak of, Thomas? The one where you are married to Ann and I to William? The one where you rise and sleep with her and your seven children? Or the one where Dorothy and I fall under William's fist before we close our eyes and as soon as we open them each day? Some life God has blessed upon me," I spit bitterly.

Thomas frowns, forcing my eyes on him as he speaks.

"The life he is blessing us now, Sarah. Our new life, our start over."

"What does thou mean? Surely you cannot speak of such things as if they are easy."

"They are not, nor will they ever be, but I will not lose the family I crave for the one I am trapped in," he says as he rests his hand onto my stomach, as if he were cradling both me and the babe with one touch.

"Thomas..."

"This is our chance, Sarah. God will look fondly upon us in bringing life into the world. He will look fondly on us doing right by this child."

"How?" I ask with a shake of my head.

He looks at me for a moment, as if he were considering our options, before he nods his head with certainty.

"We shall winter in Salem, then, with spring will come our adventure. We will take to Boston, purchase a new home, a new start."

"With what money do you speak?" I challenge.

"Mine. All of it. I'll spend every last pence if that's what it shall take."

I shake my head. "And you would leave Ann? Your children? As easy as that?"

"My children have grown to hate me at the hand of Ann, there is nothing for me here, except you," he says, rubbing his hand against my stomach.

"I won't leave Dorothy," I say.

"Nor would I expect it. She is a fine young girl. You've raised her well, and she deserves more than William could ever give. You both do."

A tear falls from my eye, this one not from pain nor sadness.

"This is madness! You do understand that, do you not?"

"That isn't a no, my love." He grins.

"Well, of course not! How could a woman refuse such an offer from the man she loves?"

Thomas's smile beams, turning to ensure we are alone before his lips meet mine. A feeling of anticipation, of excitement for what is to come, races through me as he pulls away.

"Until spring, we shall remain steadfast and strong. I shall provide whatever thou needs to keep William pacified. If he so much as lifts a finger to you, I will have no choice but to shoot him dead."

I shake my head. "I cannot ask that of you."

"You did not. I insisted upon it," he says, digging into his pocket and dropping five shillings into my hand.

"I shall bring more to the creek each week. Whatever the both of you need," he says as he looks down at my stomach.

Reluctantly, I nod.

"I...I love thee, Thomas Putnam."

"I love thee, Sarah Putnam."

My stomach flutters at his words, at the sound of our names joined together. It is a blissful sound, one I have no right to hear, yet I never want to be referred to as anything else from this day on.

Chapter Six

Thomas

My God, forgive me for what I have done, for not only have I bathed in sin, a child is now the product of our adultery. Lord, forgive me because I'm not sorry. I want her, I want them both.

Surely, I will still provide for Ann and my children. I am not a heartless man, but I have also been a hollow one for years. My own kin slowly turned against me, by their mother, no less, till I am nothing but a barely tolerated wallet for their benefits.

Sarah, though...she wants for nothing with me but...me. She craves my time, not my coin. She desires my touch, not the life I can provide. Therefore, she deserves the entire world around us. I need Sarah, not only in my life as she has been, but in my home, in my arms. Where she belongs.

The morality war raging inside me is a fierce one, there is no doubt. I may provide justifications of my *morals and actions, though I hath no doubt not another soul alive would see it through my eyes. Sarah and I would be condemned, shunned, possibly even harmed.*

I cannot let that happen. I will not.

Though I'd love nothing more than to speak with my brother or even my best friend about this, I know I ought not to. For my brother is a judgmental arse, and my best friend is the reverend of our town. Surely both would press myself to death by way of stone rather than grasp the depth of my affections for Sarah Good.

So, for now, I shall stay silent. No doubt, when spring comes along with our departure, there will be talk. There will be judgment and vile words spewed. None of that matters, though. We will be long gone, beginning our new life with my own new family, and though guilt and confliction rises inside of me, 'tis not nearly as loud or powerful of the excitement at what is to come.

Tucking away my journal, I look up from my seat in the tavern to hear a commotion occur down the road. Curious, I stand from my chair and rush outside to see Samuel screaming at the top of his lungs, his servant, Tituba, shackled in handcuffs while the sheriff marches her towards the jailhouse. The crowd around us grows by the second, and I rush forward to see what is the matter.

"Witch!" he bellows, pointing his finger at Tituba. "Vile creature of Satan! Be gone with thee! Waste not a second on this demon, Sheriff! 'Tis to the Gallows for her!"

"Sam, Sam, Sam," I say calmly, attempting to reign control over his anger.

His eyes are like fire, nostrils flared in rage as he looks to me.

"What has she done, Samuel?" I ask.

"She has bewitched my kin! Betty and Abigail are in a state of fits, uncontrollably so. They spoke of Tituba cursing them. DEVIL WOMAN!" he screams, directing that last part to her as the sheriff walks away with her.

My mind reels as I attempt to make sense of his words.

"Betty has suffered from the shaking fits since infancy, has she not?"

"Yes!" he spits. "I hath no doubt it is at the hands of Tituba that she suffers from such! Just this morning, she baked a witch cake with dear Abigail! She is a witch! What I say is the truth. All ye tread carefully!" he continues, now addressing the large crowd that has formed.

Nervous expressions splash across each of the townsfolk, soft whispers beginning as the good reverend delivers an impromptu sermon.

"You ought not forsake our Lord and Savior! For evil is among us. Cloaked in the flesh of human, the Devil has infiltrated our dear village. I hath no doubt she is not alone. There may be other devil worshipers. We must cleanse this town of their evil and eradicate it immediately. In the name of Christ our king!"

Murmurs of agreement begin to rise as the villagers become more and more agitated by each word he speaks. Uncertainty rises in me as I listen on. Witches? In Salem? For all of our sakes, I do pray he is wrong. For if an evil like that lives among us...none can be safe.

A figure catches my eye across town, and I take an opportunity in Samuel's anger to slip away. My head moves from side to side as I cross the dirt road, ensuring no prying eyes are on me. I suppose thankfully so, they are all on my best friend, whose hysterics are growing by the moment.

I follow her down the side of a building to the back alleyway. She doesn't see me coming towards her, or she hasn't a plan to stop for me. Either way, I pursue her with haste and grab her wrist when I am close enough, pushing her against the wall of the building.

A startled gasp escapes her, Sarah's eyes wide with fear until they settle on me.

"Where is thou going, my love?" I ask, softening my words as I do.

"Hello," she responds, smiling gently in a way that pulls at my heart.

"Hello," I return. "I've missed you, so."

Her smile is not nearly genuine as her gaze drifts off. The brows of my eyes pull together as I tilt her chin to face me.

"What troubles you?"

"Not a thing. Just the morning sickness and William's usual behavior."

Irritation sparks inside of me just at the mere mention of that parasite's name.

"What hath he done now? I swear to God almighty if he has touched you, I'll sooner cut off the hand that dared."

She seems pleased by my display of aggression, no doubt taking it as an act of protection. Good, as she should. That is exactly what it is. I will protect my love, my life, with everything inside of me. Especially against a simpleton drunk as William Good.

Shaking her head as to dismiss me, a smile slowly graces her face.

"He has not raised his hand against me or Dorothy. Work at the Peabody's has kept him most busy. Praise God for that. Say, what has occurred in town? I heard the reverend causing quite the stir."

I nod, looking back the way I came in case of onlookers, before my gaze returns to her.

"Tituba has been taken to the jailhouse for witchcraft."

Sarah's face turns white with fear, and I attempt to comfort her as I rest my hands onto her arms.

"Do not feel worry, my love. She has been taken care of."

She blinks for a few moments before shaking her head.

"What do you mean, witchcraft? Here? In Salem? It can't be!"

I nod. "Parris recounted Tituba has been bewitching Abigail and Betty. Believes she is to blame for Betty's shaking fits. I, too, was taken by surprise. I am heading to the jailhouse to see how I can be of assistance in the process."

Sarah does not speak, that same hollow fear staunched across her face. My hand rises to cup her cheek, my fingers tracing the smooth skin tenderly as I speak with comfort.

"Take no fear in this moment. We shall all keep the town safe, and I shall keep you safe all the same. I swear to it."

A strained smile meets her lips as she nods to me.

Looking around us once more, I ensure the coast is clear before resting my free hand onto her belly as I press my lips to hers. She meets me eagerly as our embrace becomes feverish. My hands roam over her curves as her own wrap around my neck. I ought to know better than what I am about to do, but when a woman as beautiful as Sarah looks at you and lets out the softest whimper, well, God made me only human.

My fingertips skate down her legs before pushing up her skirt. A gasp escapes her that only spurs me on. Pushing her undergarments to her knees, I'm able to pull myself from my trousers before pushing inside her. We both gasp at the feeling of being together once more. For decency, I pull her skirt down to conceal us, so that God forbid a witness should pass us by, the sight of our actions would be undetermined.

Who am I trying to fool? There would be no mistake. The joining of our bodies is hard and rough. We are not slow or subtle in our moves. I fear we will dent the brick building behind us with the fever of our thrusts.

The fear of being caught like this, with a woman who is not my wife, in public, no less, is far more thrilling than it ought to be. Dare I say, 'tis the best sex of my life. Every time with Sarah has been blissful, but this...the excitement, the rush. It is practically euphoric, and I'm a vile man for taking pleasure in such.

Her tightness grips me in a way that has myself aching for my release.

"Thomas," Sarah moans softly as I bring my free hand up to cover her mouth.

"Not a word! You should know the penalty we should face upon someone catching us like this. We'd be ruined, cast out, perhaps even tried."

"I know," she agrees as I move my hand to palm her cheek, softening her tone this time.

"Only you could do this to me, turn me into this kind of lawless, sinful man. Only you could woo me with your charm and beauty, practically forcing me to impregnate you and before you have even birthed our first child, make me desperate for another," I say between clenched teeth.

Sarah's eyes sparkle in surprise as her mouth drops open.

"Another?"

"Yes. One baby is not enough with you, Sarah. One life is not enough. The instant you are able, I will be filling you with my seed once more. Again and again until we have a brood that rivals the King of England's."

"Thomas," she cries, like my name is an answer to her prayers.

I hold her tightly, utilizing the angle of us to push myself deeper inside her.

"Nothing will ever be enough with you, my love. I want it all. We shall marry before the baby comes, so they ought not be born out of wedlock. From there, we shall start our new life, together."

"'Tis all I desire," she moans.

"I know, I know. Be my perfect girl and release for me. Allow me to fill you up so your womb shall never be empty again."

I feel her begin to clench and spasm around me before my hand presses firmly against her mouth to muffle her screams. I, too, find my release in the next moment and have no other alternative than to bury my head into her neck, sinking my teeth into her silky flesh as I fill her with my seed. As my thrusts slow, I can feel it attempt to escape her, but I will not allow it. My hips move forward several more times, ensuring every drop remains where it belongs.

We hold our embrace for several moments before I press my forehead upon hers.

"Until spring, my love," I say, rubbing my hand against our growing child.

"Until spring."

Chapter Seven

Sarah

I await for the guard to take his break before I attempt to slip into the jailhouse. Thankful to God, the sheriff has his attention on the reverend, who is still hollering and raising a commotion out front.

My feet tread carefully across the dirt floor, avoiding small puddles of water where yesterday's rain had come through the roof. The odor is repugnant in the air, stale and smelling of death. I pull my bonnet over my face, attempting to conceal my identity as I pass by a few men who are no doubt in here for various crimes, before I stop at the furthest cell around the corner.

There, Tituba sits on the floor, drawing patterns into the dirt with her finger as she murmurs something under her breath. Slowly, I lower myself to her level, tipping back my bonnet enough to allow her to see me.

"Why have you come?" she asks, her thick Caribbean accent coating her words as she keeps her eyes on the floor.

"I heard of what has happened. Tituba, you did not really bewitch those girls, I know it to be true...right?"

"Maybe. Though a little sleeping potion from time to time to calm Betty's fits. I cannot understand why the girls would turn on me so. When I have cared for them in the way their own mother cannot. Why is it so simple for them to forsake me, cast me away as if I am a danger to all?" she asks, her deep brown eyes coming to my own.

"So, you have not harmed?" I ask, making sure her intentions are pure. If they be true, there shall be no reason for this level of treatment.

A hardened look passes upon her face as she looks away and speaks.

"Perhaps a few stomach aches have been given to Elizabeth when she has treated me or the girls less than. She's a vile woman, vile things to occur to her are the least of what she deserves."

The sleep aid could be viewed as helping, though the Church and townsfolk would no doubt consider it to be witchcraft, I would like to hope they would see it for the good it is. Every time little Betty shakes, she gets slower, duller. Her body cannot take many more years of it, so I ought see nothing wrong with aiding that. 'Tis a gift if anything, but the stomach pain? Causing intentional hurt and harm? 'Tis where Tituba and I do not see eye to eye or heart to heart.

She not only practices the same healing as I, she plays in the darkness. We have not yet spoken of it deeply. For when she spoke of dolls she creates to emulate others, I insisted she stop. My mother warned me of such things as a child. A dangerous kind of power, a dark one. One that I ought not even listen to for risk spending my eternity rotting in hell with the Devil himself. She urged me to stay to the light, stay connected to God and harness the power and energy he gifted not only this world, but me with, and I have done as she so told.

"Tituba..." I trail off. "Reverend Parris is out for your head! You must stop all talk of such things," I urge as I lower my voice, fearful of the others locked away listening in.

"My head has been on his chopping block for a great long while," she says numbly, as if she has accepted the fate to come.

I roll my lips together, attempting to put into words my fears before she speaks.

"Why have you come? I know for certain, 'tis not out of concern for me."

Frowning at that, I shake my head.

"'Tis not true. I did come to see you, to discover what may have happened. To—"

"Find out if I have let on there may be more *witches* in Salem that they not know of yet?" she asks, a sharp glint in her eye as she speaks.

The way she says witches, like a hissing sound that echoes in this damp jail cell, sends chills up my back. I do not think of myself as a witch, not in the slightest. I'm a healer, a harnesser of nature. I help. I don't cast spells on people. None of that really is the point, though, is it?

"Please, Tituba. I'm begging. I have a child. I...I'm with child," I say a little softer.

That appears to grip hold of her attention. Her head turns up with haste as she looks at me curiously before her dirt covered hand reaches through the jail bars, landing right onto my stomach. She closes her eyes, inhaling deeply before she pulls away. Her eyes open, and her hand leaves behind a near perfect handprint onto my dress as a sinister smile spreads across her face.

"And 'tis not your husband's child."

She tuts at me as if I am a misbehaving child as she shakes her head.

"You have been a naughty witch, Miss Sarah."

"I am not a witch," I hiss under my breath. "You ought not be spreading lies of good people! What have I ever done to deserve that kind of betrayal? I have aided you when you have asked of it. I

have created tonics, fetched herbs when you could not. We were...
we are friends, are we not?"

Tituba sits back, resting her head against the cement wall.

"Only in namesake. I hath not spoken your name or others out
of loyalty. Yet."

"What do you mean, yet?" I ask, fear shaking through my voice
as I lean in closer. "Are you threatening me?"

"No, Miss Sarah...but in these times...I will do what is necessary for my survival."

Fear clenches inside me as I stand, covering my face once more
as I run out of the jailhouse, slipping out the back as I did in. I do
not stop running till I am all the way home. Once I arrive, I have
every intention of packing anything I can carry for myself and
Dorothy and running. Where, I cannot be sure, but...anywhere.
Then I think on what will cross Thomas's mind when he discovers
I've run away, with his baby. He will come for me, chase me, and
bring the Church right along with him. Closing my eyes, I make a
plan. I will find him tomorrow. I will convince him of my terror
with the whispers of witches, with the danger to Dorothy and our
baby. I will urge us to make the journey now. Winter or not, if I do
not leave Salem soon, I fear I will not live to see the next.

Chapter Eight

Thomas

I find myself unable to take my mind off Sarah. She wholly occupies my mind and all my heart desires. I wish nothing more than to be by her side now as spring draws near. The preparations have been made, our time is growing near. Two more Sundays and the journey shall be more favorable for young Dorothy as well as Sarah in her condition. Her belly grows by the day, as does my joy. She believes it to be a little girl and was worried that would displease me. Maybe at times it would, but not with her, nothing with her could ever bring me anything but happiness.

Instead of preparing my fresh start, tidying up my affairs, or sneaking in a few more minutes with my beloved, I am here, in the town's meetinghouse, where we are finally interrogating Tituba for her crimes against Parris's daughter and niece.

He has been beside himself with anger, desperate to try her for her wrongdoing, but it had taken time to assemble everyone for a proper interrogation in the dead of winter.

Jonathon Corwin calls attention to the room before the jailer brings in Tituba. Her ankles and wrists are shackled, her feet bare, and her face lacking any real emotion as she stares at each one of us assembled in the meetinghouse. When her eyes land on me, goose-bumps appear across my skin, and I do not like it at all.

"Tituba, I think you ought know why you have been taken under arrest," Corwin begins.

"I know what you all try to besmirch my name with," she agrees.

"Are you saying it is not the truth Reverend Parris speaks?" John Hathorne asks from the corner of the room.

"Liar! She is a liar and an enchantress! Can you not all see? The culture she brings to our pure village, it tarnishes our life, our children. I place the blame on my own household for allowing it here this long. We must purge Salem of this evil at once!" Parris exclaims, jumping to his feet as murmurs echo in the room.

"Tituba?" Hathorne asks, directing his attention to the woman in question instead of our impassioned reverend.

"I have never *caused* the shaking fits of Miss Betty."

"But is thou a witch? Does thou perform witchcraft? Is your loyalty to the Devil himself, or Jesus Christ?" My brother intervenes from my right.

Tituba sets her sights onto my brother, that same hollow look upon her face as she takes him in and shakes her head.

"I do not accept your notions of religion, for they go against my own."

"Do you hear that? She rejects our lord and savior! She is evil incarnate!" Parris begins again.

I frown at her words, as do many of the others, as Hathorne continues his interrogations.

"You reject the Church, but you are not a witch? Is that what you speak?"

"I do not claim such title," she speaks cryptically.

Hathorne's patience wanes as he glances to the guard, nodding his head. In the next moment, a club is pulled from beside him as he hits her across the back. She cries out in pain, falling to the floor as he strikes her again and again. The scent of blood fills the meet-inghouse, sickening my stomach with each blow, before Hathorne makes a ceasing motion with his hand.

The guard hauls a bloody Tituba to her feet, face to face with Hathorne as he speaks.

"I grow tired of your games. Speak truth in this moment, does thou practice magic?"

She remains silent for a moment before a sickening smile spreads across her face, blood spilling down her lip as she speaks.

"I do."

"She admits it! Straight to the Gallows with you! Jailer, take her immediately to Gallows Hill," Parris begins.

I rest my hand onto his arm, attempting to settle him. His eyes turn to me with outrage, but 'tis enough to keep him silent as Corwin speaks.

"Agreed. We have no room in our perfect new world for the likes of you. Your evil may have originated elsewhere, but it will soon die as it ought."

The jailer begins to take Tituba away as an evil laugh bubbles through her chest.

"Hang me at the Gallows, I have little care, but your troubles are far from over."

"What does thou mean?" I sneer.

Tituba's devilish smile turns to my own as she shakes her head, her lips sealed. Unrest begins stirring amongst the men as chatter rises.

"Does she mean there are more witches? In Salem?"

"Surely not!"

"Bring in the girls!" another exclaims.

Corwin attempts to control the room, but it is hardly success-ful. Glancing to Parris, he nods his agreement. I hear Parris curse beneath his breath, a thing I have never heard escape my friend's mouth as he storms out of the meetinghouse to fetch his kin.

When I turn back to face the room, I find Tituba's eyes on me once more, that evil grin with a curious glint in her eyes. It unnerves me immensely, though I do not allow it to show.

Within the hour, Parris is back, accompanied by young Betty and Abigail, who look sickly and disturbed, visibly shaking when they enter the same room as their assumed tormentor.

"Girls, what treatment have ye experienced?" Corwin asks them.

They look fearful as their eyes bounce around the room.

"We have been bitten and pinched!" Abigail cries.

"And tortured as well!" Betty agrees.

"By whom?" Hathorne asks.

"Tituba, of course!" Betty exclaims.

"Anyone else?" Parris asks. "We have reason to believe of others in Salem, think long on it. Who else torments thee?"

The girls exchange looks and softened whispers before Parris presses on.

"For all to hear! Who torments you?"

"Tituba, Sarah Osborne, and Sarah Good!"

Outrage flies around the room as I feel my heart cease beating. My whole body goes numb and cold before I jump to my feet.

"Outrageous! Where are the facts of your claims? How do we know they have not pulled these names from thin air? Brothers, we must tread carefully with accusations of such."

"What say you all the same?" Corwin challenges. "We may be dealing with an issue greater than one or three witches, Putnam. Do you have any proof or fact to soil the claims of these victims?"

I want to say yes, to tell them my Sarah would never hurt another. She is quiet and impoverished with a sad excuse of a husband. She is not well liked because of him and the things he forces her to do, yet none of this means she is evil. She loves God as I do. She loves her daughter, her town. She is no more a witch than

I, but I ought know better than to speak such things nor raise suspicions.

"We need to examine them too!" my brother exclaims, casting me a suspicious look as others cheer in agreement.

My eyes widen in panic at the idea of such, but I remain calm and steady as I agree.

"Let us gather them at once and examine for truth. Just as you speak, Corwin, if the claims are true, who is to say it ends with three? All of Salem may be in danger of purgatory if we do not move with haste."

Corwin nods, as does Hathorne.

"Go forth, gather the two women and bring them at once. We shall hold a town meeting this Sunday."

"I will collect Osborne, her shop lay beside my tavern," Ingersoll says.

"I will accompany thee." Parris nods.

"I shall collect Good," I volunteer.

"Then I too shall accompany you, brother," Edward speaks.

I lower my voice for us two only.

"That need not be necessary. I can manage such matters."

"I have no doubt in that, brother, but I shall accompany you regardless."

My eyes shoot daggers towards him, but I make haste out the door before others should try to follow. When I suggested to bring them in, my first thought was to grab Sarah and run. Hide her in the woods if I must until nightfall. Edward has made this matter all the more complicated now, and I'm not so sure of what my actions will be next.

My boots crush the dirt beneath me as I all but run to the Good home. Edward is quick to keep beside me, his words harsh and brash.

"Whatever is the hurry? Surely, she is not going anywhere."

"I want justice for Salem and security at once," I speak, not turning around to look him in the eye.

He does not respond, though I know that is trouble. Edward surely always has something on his mind, and when he remains silent, it is when the thoughts run rampant in his head.

My heart plummets when we arrive at the Good house to see Sarah and Dorothy out front. They are laughing, spinning in circles filled with joy. I so wish she had been away.

They both notice me, Sarah's smile on me for a moment before it drops at the sight of Edward.

"Mr. Putnam and Mr. Putnam," she greets.

"You need to come with me, Mrs. Good. Now," I say, attempting to sound as authoritative as possible.

Fear flashes upon her features as she tucks Dorothy behind her. "Whatever for?"

"There are claims against you. You are required to appear before the town this Sunday," Edward speaks.

"Claims?" she asks as her husband steps outside.

"What is the meaning of your trespass?" he slurs, his stance wavering as he does.

The drunk arse is worse off than I ever knew. The stories Sarah has told me ignite my soul with a burning anger that will only have relief when William Good is cold and rotting beneath the earth. I do not have a moment to channel any ire to him. Instead, I have only one to think of.

"Witchcraft," Edward says, startling William. "Your wife has been accused of bewitching two young girls. We've been sent to fetch her for examination."

William turns to face Sarah, rearing back his hand to deliver a blow to her face. I do not allow it, though. I step in between them, catching his arm easily as I toss it to the side.

"You shall not touch her. She is needed in town. You may be allowed visitations after she is seen."

Like hell I would allow such things.

William scoffs. "Why would I want to see her? Take her from my sight, banish her, hang her for all I care. Devil woman, curse of my life!" he shouts, spitting at her feet.

I turn to face Sarah, who has gone white in the face. She turns to run, and I make no effort to grab her. Unfortunately, Edward does. He sees her eagerness to flee and grabs her up in the next moment.

"NO! Let me go! 'Tis a lie! I am but innocent! Nooo!" she screams as Edward hauls her towards the road.

My heart cracks in half at the sounds of her screams as little Dorothy chases after them.

"Mama! Mama!"

I stop her quickly, kneeling down to speak to her.

"Please, do not follow us, Dorothy. Everything will be as it should. I promise."

She looks up at me, tear filled eyes so full of fear. I have yet to spend time with this child, though I have promised Sarah to care for her like my own. In this moment, she feels more like my own than any of my real children do.

"Stay, please. I will take care of us," I say softly, only for her little ears.

She looks confused at my words but nods as she watches Edward carry on, hauling her mother down the road. I hurry after them, casting Dorothy one last look as tears pour down her sweet face.

Once I catch up to them, I pull Sarah from Edward's grasp immediately. Edward attempts to steal her from me as I shove him away. He looks at me with outrage.

"What is the matter, brother? Want the witch all to yourself?"

I sneer at him, tightening my hold on her.

"That be enough out of you. There be only claims had, no proof. We were sent to collect for examination. That is it."

Edward mutters something beneath his breath that I cannot quite make out. I do not pay him any mind either as I look to Sarah, allowing us to walk ahead of Edward so we may speak to one another.

"What is going on, Thomas? I'm frightened."

"You have nothing to be frightened of. The Parris girls have made claims against a few. Your innocence will shine through."

She swallows roughly, her limbs shaking in my hold as we continue down the road. God, please let this nonsense be put to rest. I know not what Corwin or Hathorne have planned, but I pray it is quick, easy, and allows Sarah and I to escape this village in one piece. Together.

Chapter Nine

Sarah

I stand in Ingersoll's tavern still and in waiting. I had to spend the night in the jailhouse, which was cold, damp, and so very unnerving. Tituba, Sarah Osborne, and I all stand shoulder to shoulder, though I cannot look at either. I fear to incriminate myself, or worse, stoke anger in them. I do not believe it for a moment that the Parris girls are to blame for my involvement. Tituba all but threatened me. Sarah...well, she is one of the only people in Salem to know of my gifts, and the way she shakes tells me she will spill all of them to protect herself.

Over a dozen men line the walls as John Hathorne and Jonathon Corwin "examine" us.

"There be a witch among you three, do not try to deny it. Come forth of ye wrongdoings, and you shall receive protection," Corwin speaks.

"Protection?" Osborne questions.

"Hathorne and I have agreed to offer dismissal for anyone who accepts the charge of witch and agrees to never again practice such sinful things."

"As well as assisting us in sorting out any other witches that may lie in the village," Hathorne adds.

"I object! I object strongly!" Reverend Parris thunders.

"This not be a court of law, but if it were, thou hast no authority. Stand down, Samuel," Corwin speaks.

Parris crosses his arms similarly to how my Dorothy does when she is not able to get her way. I hear him grumble under his breath, his eyes like fire as they rake over each of us.

I stay silent, for I ought know better than to make a deal with the likes of them. Especially when what they say is not true. I am no witch. I have never cursed nor bewitched anyone. I heal; I help. I harness the gifts and energy God has graced our lands with. 'Tis not a crime, at least it ought not be. I do not worship the Devil or any of the theories these men have conjured in their minds. 'Tis not who I am, and I shall not cower to their threats, nor besmirch myself for falsities.

"I am a witch," Tituba speaks, forcing my head to swing towards her in surprise.

"I knew it!" Parris exclaims.

"What about you? You?" Hathorne asks Osborne and I.

We both shake our heads, and he lets out a heavy sigh.

"Take Tituba back to the jail for now. Good, Osborne, undress."

"What?" Osborne exclaims. "For what purpose?"

"To check ye over for witch's teats. You heard the man," Corwin says.

I shake my wrists together, attempting to silently remind the thick heads that even if we wanted to, we have no ability to do such things when we are shackled like prisoners.

Corwin's eyes snap down to them as he nods to himself as if he thought of it.

"Undo their chains and remove their clothes, let us not leave an inch unturned."

"I have no such things!" Osborne exclaims.

"Nor does Good," Thomas speaks, though I cringe as he does. What a foolish man.

All eyes swing to him as Ingersoll begins undoing my chains and then Osborne's.

"And how can you know that for certain?" Parris questions him.

Thomas does not falter, remaining steadfast in his confidence.

"Would we not have seen it already? We know this to be true; witches are the ugliest of lot. The darkness inside them rots them on the outside like a bad apple. Surely, we'd have already seen a witch's teat if it lay there, no?"

"You heard Corwin, brother, we must be thorough," Edward Putnam smirks as he comes to me, his repulsive fingers quickly undoing my buttons.

Anger slashes across Thomas's face as he approaches his brother, shoving him towards Osborne as he takes his place. I can feel the difference in Thomas's touch. 'Tis soft, gentle, begging for forgiveness with each brush. No amount of forgiveness can absorb the humiliation that consumes me as the cold air nips at my bare skin.

Several men whistle and clap in celebration as Osborne and I stand bare.

"Spread them!" a man calls out from the back, rewarded with a ruckus of cheers.

Edward smirks as he reaches around Sarah, lifting each breast to show the lot, not before he pinches her nipple hard, even sucking one into his mouth. I cringe at the horrific act as Thomas does the same to me, but with dignity. He quickly and thoroughly lifts my breasts, proving there be no sign of a witch's teat. They look for anything from a large freckle or mark, even a third nipple. I already know to be true I have none, though.

When Edward bends Sarah over before spreading her bottom, I

know what shall come next for me. Thomas looks at me with regret, speaking feather light as he pushes me down.

"Close your eyes, my love. We're nearly done."

A tear rolls down my face as I do what he commands, and I do not open my eyes until I feel the familiarity of my clothes being wrapped back around me. Thomas's nimble fingers quickly button me up, resting a comforting hand upon my lower back before stepping away.

"No teats, as I said."

"Aye," Edward agrees. "Though I quite enjoyed that," he says with a salacious lick of his lips.

More laughter and cheers erupt as Corwin shakes his head like he is in on the fun. I look to see Osborne half dressed before Ingersoll is shackling her once more. Tears are streaming down her face, and despite our past, all I care to do is comfort her in this moment.

"Bring in the girls," Hathorne says.

A door is opened, and little Betty Parris and Abigail Williams walk into the tavern. They are clinging to one another like they are struck with fear, but I cannot for the life of me fathom why.

"Girls, are these your tormentors?" Parris asks them.

Both of their eyes come to mine, and I see the truth in an instant. Betty looks truly frightened, sharing nervous looks with her cousin. Abigail, though, her fear is a farce. A smile is pulling at the corners of her mouth like she is playing a game.

"Yes!" Abigail screams. "They have pinched us and scratched us. See?" she says, exposing her arms that bear deep red scratches.

I withhold the roll of my eyes at her nonsense; they cannot believe such lies. They can, though. The men are impassioned with anger as they glare at Osborne and myself. I am not the only one outraged by the falsities, though. To my left, I hear near silent murmuring. My eyes move to see Osborne's mouth moving as she stares at the young girls, especially Abigail. Osborne's mouth moves faster and faster as that playful smile on Abigail's face disappears, her mouth shaping an "O" as she screams in pain. Abigail drops to the floor, clutching her belly as she begins to scream.

"What has happened?" the reverend shouts in a panic.

Osborne's head turns to face Betty before she, too, drops to the floor.

My eyes round with understanding. Sarah Osborne. She harnesses the dark magic. I never knew this. How did I not know?

"She's a witch," I say to myself, unaware it slipped from my mouth before Edward speaks.

"What? What did thee say!?"

"Witch! She said witch, I heard her true as day!" Thomas Preston shouts.

William Griggs, the town's doctor, rushes to the girls, giving them what appears to be a quick examination before looking to us both.

"Witches! They have bewitched the girls for the truth they speak!"

Unrest erupts as bodies begin shoving and pushing into us. Fists are flying and several land upon me. I cry out before I feel a pair of hands tug me to the side. Thomas.

"Enough! This shall not be how we conduct so. Good spoke out against Osborne, surely that provides immunity per thy terms?" he barters.

The crowd settles and nods as Osborne looks to be with outrage.

"Yet she be the biggest witch of all! She provides my shop with tonics and remedies she creates through witchcraft!"

I look at her in outrage as she continues on.

"I have seen it! She conjures spells and places magic on all she touches!"

The crowd becomes restless once more, pushing and shoving Osborne and I before Corwin and Hathorne intervene.

"That be the end of it! Enough! Sarah Good, Sarah Osborne, ye both are hereby under arrest for suspicion of witchcraft. You shall be granted a hearing when we are able to gather such. Till then, you shall remain at the jail in Ipswich. Take them away!"

Hands grab me, ripping me out of the tavern. I scream and fight against their hold as I'm dragged out to the street, tossed to the ground like a heap of waste. I clutch my growing belly with protection as pain fills me.

Thomas rushes over, crouching down to help me stand.

"My love, are you hurt?" he asks, his hand resting upon my belly.

"Thomas! What do I do?" I cry.

"Do as they say. We will sort this," he assures. "We will prove your innocence."

I open my mouth to tell him that I'm not innocent, though. What Osborne spoke was the truth, but there is more to it than such. Thomas sees the confliction on my face and frowns, as if he can read my own mind.

Phillip Lewis walks by us, holding onto Osborne as he forces her onto his horse before climbing on behind her.

"Come on, Putnam. I want to be off. The sooner we jail them, the better."

Thomas looks like he is wavering on his next move when I am ripped from Thomas's grasp.

"Not a worry, Lewis. Walcott will take Good. My brother and I have matters to handle," Edward says as Jonathan Walcott takes hold of me, forcing me up onto a horse before he climbs on himself.

Before Thomas can object, we are off at a gallop. I turn to see Edward holding Thomas back, shouting into his face. Thomas's eyes do not leave my own until we round the corner. The fear, anxiety, and turmoil swirling inside me is almost too much to handle as I bounce upon the horse. What a rough ride it will be for the ten mile ride to Ipswich. All I can manage to think about is my Dorothy, the baby in my belly, and...Thomas.

Chapter Ten

Thomas

"What are you doing?" Edward screams in my face.

I reel back at the anger in his tone.

"What am I doing? What are you? Why did you send her off with Walcott of all people? The man is an arse!"

"Why are you concerned where or with whom a *witch* goes?"

My eyes narrow at him as I lower my tone.

"She is not a witch."

"Then what is she, brother? Is she your whore? The bed too cold with Ann at nights, so you took a fancy with the beggar woman. Please tell me she parts her legs better than her lazy husband work—"

He does not get to finish his sentence before my fist is driving into his face. He staggers backwards, blood beginning to run down his face as I take hold of his jacket, pulling him close to my face.

"Speak ill of her again, and I shall slit your throat myself. Mention her body in any such way, and I shall shoot you dead. Do not try my patience, brother, if I must choose between her or you, it shall be her. Every. Time."

Edward looks speechless, whether from shock or rage, I cannot be sure. I imagine he was throwing guesses, but did not think I would confess to my feelings. What do I have to lose in the name of things at the moment? My world is falling apart, the woman I love, pregnant with my child, has been arrested for witchcraft, and I am unsure how I will free her from such a situation. One thing is true. I must get to the bottom of this, speak with her, do anything and everything I am able to set us both free. 'Tis the only way.

Moving away from Edward, I take to my horse across the way. I ready her for the ride as Edward shouts at me from across town.

"So that is it? Thou follows her like a good servant? Is she your master?"

Yes. Master of my heart, of my happiness, of my world. I do not wish to care how that makes me sound. How backwards that may be. I love her, and I will live for her until my dying breath.

I pay no mind to my infuriating brother as I ride in the direction to Ipswich. I cannot take a full breath until I see her once more, until I sort this matter. I have never come upon an issue that money or influence could not resolve. I anticipate this matter to be just the same.

I made the ride to Ipswich in good time. Good enough that as I was arriving, Walcott and Lewis were leaving back to Salem. Both exchanged curious glances with each other before casting their looks my way, but, nevertheless, they rode on.

I jump down to my feet, securing my horse, and step inside the jail. 'Tis as if I can already feel her presence here. Like the uncertainty inside me settles when I am near her. The jailor looks upon me with irritation.

"What business does thou have?"

"I shall first require you to adjust your tone when you speak to me in such a manner," I snarl.

The young lad who ought not be older than twenty rights himself but looks to me with unease as I continue.

"My name is Thomas Putnam, I am one of the most prominent members of Salem Village, and I will be treated as such, or it shall be your job, perhaps even your head, if you wish to continue."

'Tis arrogant of me to expect such treatment from someone who hath never met me. Perhaps even more so to assume he knows of me, though my reputation appears to not have let me down just yet. At the sound of my name, the young jailor seems to pale and swallow.

"Mr. Putnam, apologies. I did not know."

"And now you do. Forget your hollow words and listen carefully as I speak. I am here on urgent business. I must speak with one of the accused you have in your custody. Sarah Good."

He nods, moving to guide me down to the jail cells.

I must admit, I did not think it would be that easy.

When he reaches the end of the cells, I see Sarah sitting upon the dirt covered floor in the corner. Beside her sits Sarah Osborne, though neither gazes upon one another. My love looks to me, hope blooming in her tear filled eyes as the jailor nods to her.

"This be the one, sir?"

"Aye," I agree as I look down at her, doing my best to mask my desire. "Does thou possess an interrogation room here?"

"No, sir. Not as of yet."

I purse my lips. I really ought to have wished for privacy, especially from Osborne.

"The nature of which I speak has no business for prying ears," I say to him, gesturing to Osborne.

She shoots me a dirty look that I barely acknowledge. The jailor nods as he unlocks the door and steps inside, grabbing Osborne's shackled hands before dragging her to her feet.

"This one could use a bucket of water. Not even in her cell for an hour and already stunk up the place."

I nod, not giving a damn what he does with her as long as he takes her away. I do not move an inch till I hear the sound of the door shutting before stepping into the cell, dropping to my knees beside Sarah. Her arms embrace me, and I press my lips to her own before I can take my next breath. Finally. Peace. It washes over me like a fresh wave, breathing life into my starved soul. I hold us in place for what feels like eternity, and yet, not at all long enough.

When we break apart, a sadness fills me as I take in the conditions in which she endures.

"Why have you come? Will others not talk?" Sarah asks.

"Allow them to do so. I shall not care for their hollow words. I need only hear the truth in thine."

She frowns at me and shakes her head.

"What do you speak of?"

I swallow, not wanting to speak my thoughts aloud. Once I do, they are out there for good, and I am too fearful of the answer. I love the woman before me, there be no doubt of that, I also have come to know her well during our courtship. Well, enough to know when there is more to a story, more that she has yet to share, and I fear that is the case.

"The nonsense Osborne spoke of...about you. Give me the words I need to defend you. Speak the truth, they were falsities, yes?"

Understanding comes upon her face, twisting my stomach with nerves.

"Thomas..." she speaks softly.

My name. Not a yes. Not an explanation. A plea.

Slowly, I withdraw my hands from hers as I stand to my feet. I pace in place for several moments before turning to look down upon her.

"'Tis true? You are a witch?"

"NO! No," she says as she climbs to her feet, attempting to convince me. "I am not what they say, nor have I done what I am accused of. I..." She pauses for a moment, rubbing her lips together as if they will do the speaking for her.

"I am no witch, Thomas. I love God and reject the Devil. I love you. I would never lie to you, about anything."

"But you certainly withheld this for the duration of our courtship, did you not?" I snap, fury and betrayal coursing through my veins as I look upon the woman I thought I knew better than myself.

She looks hurt, in response to my words or maybe my tone, as she shakes her head.

"I've never spoken aloud of what I practice. I knew how the Church would see it, how people would talk. I am not evil. I only try to bring good. I harness the energy and gifts God has provided me to do good. Tonics, supplements, healing stones. I do not channel dark, only light. I have never afflicted anyone nor harmed in any way. Thomas, please, you know me," she begs.

I shake my head, staring at the cement wall as I mull over her words. They pull at my heart the way all her words do. I want so badly to believe her, to trust her. How can what she say be true? A good witch? A light witch? There be no such thing. Though if there ever would be, I imagine she would look something like my Sarah. Kind, warm, giving.

"Speak true to me now, did you harm Abigail or Betty?"

"No!" she insists. "I never cross paths with the girls. When would I have the time nor desire to do such things?"

I watch her closely, searching for a hint of insincerity in her words, but I come up shy. She seems to be speaking the truth, and I want to believe her, so. There is a small voice in the back of my head that screams for me to tread with caution. Whether it be the little angel or devil on either shoulder, I cannot speak on which calls to me now.

Shaking my head, I look to the ground as I speak, not having the gall to do it eye to eye.

"I think 'tis best you stay here till evidence can be collected."

"As if I had a choice," she scoffs. "Say what you truly mean, Thomas. You believe me not, and now you are turning thy back upon me. Upon us," she says, resting her shackled hands upon her belly.

That stirs something inside me, and I close the distance between us, placing my hands on top of hers.

"Never. I just...I am worried if they speak the truth, my love. I have faith in you, but others will not. Maybe...maybe you ought confess to witchcraft as Tituba did. She is being gifted pardon in exchange."

"No. I will not allow them to depict me for something I am not."

I attempt to reason with her. "Sarah, thee will not stand a fair trial! If thou tries to explain you are a good sort of witch, they will remain unbelieving and you will hang!"

"Do not forsake my intelligence, Thomas. They will hang me either way."

"No," I say, clenching my teeth together. "No. I will not allow it. We will...will find a way. I will break thee out of here. I shall head back to Salem Village, collect provisions, and will return for you in a fortnight."

"What of Dorothy?" she argues.

"My concern is getting you away from danger first. We will fetch Dorothy at a later time. Stay safe. I will return soon."

She blinks up at me with uncertainty when the sound of the door echoes through the jail. Hurriedly, I press a kiss to her lips as she whispers.

"Do not forget me."

"Never," I vow as I slip out of the cell, attempting to mask my emotions as the jailor brings in a dripping wet Osborne.

He tosses her into the cell, locking it behind her as he looks to me.

"Is thy business concluded?"

"For now." I nod as I begin walking with the jailor towards the door. "We are taking a special interest in Mrs. Good. We believe she could be a key witness in aiding our efforts. I need you to take special care of her. Treat the others how you may, but not a scratch upon her. Do you understand?" I ask, fishing out a small bag that holds ten shillings.

I drop the bag into the jailor's hand, and his eyes widen.

"O-of course, sir."

"And see to it she receives extra food and water rations. She is with child."

"Yes, Mr. Putnam."

I nod, shaking his hand before stepping outside the jailhouse, my chest aching with each step away from her I take.

March 11th, 1692

The desire to be near her is near agonizing. It has been just five days, yet it feels as if weeks. Nine more nights until everything changes. I will no doubt be a wanted man for my actions. Others will never understand, nor attempt to, and the hysteria of Salem grows by the day. I know not what to tell Ann and the children, if anything at all. I must admit, under the warm summer nights in Sarah's embrace, the plan to run had such an allure, but feels tainted with guilt and shame in the light of day.

For what kind of man am I to consider such

things? Abandon an entire family for a woman akin to a witch? A good one says she, but a witch all the same. 'Tis an outrage. I can feel God's judgment already, yet this time, I am unable to delude myself into believing I shall earn his forgiveness so easily.

"Thomas! Thomas! Come quick!" Ann shouts, running into the room.

I look up from my pages, snapping my journal closed as I jump to my feet.

"What is it?" I ask.

"'Tis Ann! Something is wrong," she says, leading me to the sitting room where our daughter is convulsing onto the floor in what appears to be a fit.

Panic rises inside me as I drop to the ground and attempt to hold her still. Her mouth emits a pained screech as her body continues to shake before she stops.

"Fetch Griggs! Hurry!" I snap at my wife.

She nods quickly and runs out the door in the next moment.

"Ann, Ann, Ann," I say, shaking her softly before her eyes blink up to me.

"Father?" she questions, as if she has been trapped in another place.

"What happened to you, child?"

"I...I do not know. I ate some berries Mother and I purchased from Martha Corey, and...has she cursed me, Father?" she asks, fear heavy in her eyes.

Berries? From the Corey farm? They provide half the town with their provisions of berries. Surely it ought not be such a sinister cause. Then again, the entirety of Salem is not as it was. Anything may be possible, and if the Coreys are poisoning, any and all...

Could it be? Another witch among us? It ought not be...though if my Sarah could be one, who is to say anyone else is innocent?

Griggs and Ann rush in the next minute, quickly examining her. Ann recounts their morning to Griggs as he listens intently.

"What say you?" I ask him.

He shakes his head. "She appears fine now, nothing of physical nature appears wrong. Which means..." He trails off as his eyes hold my own, a silent conversation held between us as I nod my head and stand to my feet. I grab my hat, slipping it upon my head as my wife calls out to me.

"Wherever are you heading?"

"To the Corey's farm," I say stiffly.

As I step out of my house and down the road, I see my brother tending to his yard.

"What is the fuss over there?"

"Come," I bark, my strides purposeful and long.

He does as I speak, dropping his tool as he joins me on my walk.

"Where are we heading?"

"To seek out Martha Corey," I speak.

"For what purpose?"

"She has afflicted my daughter, Ann. Poisoned her with berries."

"Another witch? Are you certain?" Edward asks.

I look to him with a shake of my head.

"I am not certain of anything any longer."

Martha was easy to find. She tended to her garden as if nothing was amiss. Edward and I left her little choice. He wrenched her up and threw her over his shoulder, hauling her to town as her husband,

Giles, ran a fit. I warned him he ought not get in the way of village business, and he finally allowed us to leave.

We dropped Martha off with Reverend Noyes, Corwin, and Hathorne to be interrogated at the jailhouse before heading to Ingersoll's. The pint before me remains untouched as I sit with Edward, Ingersoll, Preston, and Parris.

"We will be praying for your Ann's recovery, Thomas," Parris says.

"Thank you, Samuel."

"I fear this be but the start," he continues.

"What do you mean by the words you speak?" Preston asks.

"But a fortnight ago, the idea of witches in Salem was mad. Now...I fear the worst."

"As do I," Edward jumps in.

Parris nods like he appreciates the support as he continues.

"We must protect Salem as best as we are able, our souls are depending on it. We must honor and serve God, seeking out evil and banishing it at first bloom."

The others nod their heads as indecision wavers through me. Their words speak to the truth inside me. I know it to be true. Evil is among us, and 'tis coming for our children first. I stay silent because what words do I speak? The very thing we talk of destroying lives inside the one soul who truly calls to me. Or is that part of it all? Has it been a guise from the very beginning? An intention, a trick, a spell?

I so desperately want to think naught of it, but how can I not consider the possibility? I know not of Sarah's limitations, nor her darkest thoughts. For all I know, she has been planning to seduce me for quite some time, and I was the fool to fall for her tricks.

No.

That doesn't feel right, though. My heart and head cannot agree on such. So, I remain quiet while the others plot to seek out any and all wrongdoers. Instead, I remain at war with myself and what I am to do.

Chapter Eleven

Sarah

A fortnight came and went, but Thomas did not. On the first day of his expected arrival, I was hopeful and ready. By the second day, I was concerned something happened to him. By the third, I was smart enough to understand things clearly. He wasn't coming for me. Fear, ignorance, or maybe something in between, has warped his mind, and he has abandoned me, perhaps even forgotten. The truth of that hurts more than any blow from William's hand ever could.

More have been arrested and brought here since mine and Osborne's arrival, and I fear 'tis only the beginning. When the sound of the door opening echoes throughout this morbid place, I don't pay too much mind to it. Until I hear a familiar cry. Leaping to my feet, I press myself against the bars as I see Dorothy in shackles, crying as she is being carried down the hall.

"Dorothy! Dorothy!"

The jailer is carrying her to another cell as I shout for him.

"Please! Please, allow her into here. 'Tis my child!"

He looks back at me with a sneer, ready to refuse me until his eyes meet my own. I am unsure of what Thomas said to him, but whatever he did, it has afforded me better treatment from the young jailer than most. I suppose I have something to thank him for...only this, though.

Turning, he approaches my cell, opening the door and tossing her inside. I catch her easily, wrapping my arms around her as she sobs into my neck.

"Mama! Is that you?"

"Yes, baby. 'Tis me. Are you hurt?"

She shakes her head as her beautiful eyes come to mine.

"I missed you, Mama."

Clutching her tighter to me, I rock us slowly.

"I missed you too. We're together now. All is well."

She sniffs hard before resting her hand upon my stomach.

"I missed the baby too."

Pain runs through my chest, though I do not allow it to show. Nodding my head, she curls up into my lap as we sit there for many moments.

"Mr. Putnam was right."

I frown as I look down at her.

"About what?"

"When they took you, he promised everything would be as it should. That he would take care of us."

"Does it look like he has done such, Dorothy? We are in jail. I can only imagine you are here for the same as I. We are in danger, sweetheart."

She shrugs. "But I am with you, Mama. As it should be."

Something about my sweet girl's words warms me, so. Not enough to thaw to Putnam. Regardless of the words he gave her, I know now he never meant them. Never intended to keep true to his word. Even if he did, he's a coward, and we are better off without him. At least, that is what I try to tell myself. It helps temper the sting of betrayal.

I'm unsure of the day, what does it matter, honestly? The rations are abysmal, apart from my own, which I suspect is due to Thomas. Any extras I receive go to Dorothy, and thankfully, she has kept weight well as with her spirit. We are playing a game, clapping our hands together, when Joseph Hutchinson and Phillip Lewis appear before us. Carefully, I tuck Dorothy behind me, concerned they have come for her as the jailer opens the door. Hutchinson reaches down for me, and I go easily, though I lose my footing for a moment with my growing belly. Oh, how my body hurts from days of sleeping on this hard dirt floor.

"Stand up," he snaps before the jailer shuts the door behind us.

"Mama!" Dorothy calls out in a panic.

"'Tis alright, sweetheart. Come up with another game. I will return shortly."

Lewis scoffs under his breath as they escort me outside.

"Do not count upon it."

His words send a chill through me as we approach the two horses. I expect them to throw me upon one as they did in town, but instead, they latch a chain to my shackles as they both mount their horses. I look up at Hutchinson in confusion as he jerks on the chain.

"Make haste, witch! We haven't all day."

They expect me to walk? Both ways? 'Tis ten miles each, at the least, and my feet are but bare. I resist only for a moment before the chain forces me to comply or risk being dragged. I wince as we cross a few twigs and sharp bushes; each step forces my feet to ache and burn until eventually, I do not feel them at all.

I never thought I'd feel relief returning to Salem. Though I imagine I have not been away for longer than a month, with the spring in full bloom, it feels like such a long time ago that I was last here. My feet barely stop by themselves as we halt outside the courthouse. I half expected us to return to Ingersoll's once more. Though it seems I am being taken in for trial or questioning, I ought not be too sure. Perhaps 'tis in my favor that it is being done in a formal setting. Perhaps justice will prevail, and the truth shall be revealed.

Hutchinson yanks on the chain attached to my shackles as he pulls me forward, towards the courthouse. As soon as Lewis opens the large wooden doors, I'm greeted with a musty odor that is foul to the senses. My eyes move around the room to see most of the village gathered, many casting scornful looks my way, as I count nine men sitting at the front of the room, all staring at me with watchful eyes. I recognize Corwin and Hathorne, but the rest are strangers to me.

As I am escorted to the front, I am unable to miss his gaze on me. As if I can feel it rather than see it. Turning my head, I lock eyes with Thomas. The instant I do, he drops his head, as if he doesn't wish to glance my way. I feel my heart crack inside my chest while his wife rests her hand onto his, sneering at me in disgust. Hurt and anger mix inside me as I face forward.

"Let the record show that I, William Stroughton, Chief Justice of the Court of Oyer and Terminer, hereby appointed by Governor Phips, declare the commencement of this trial against one Sarah Good," the man in the middle speaks.

"Mrs. Good, how do you plead?" Corwin asks.

"Plead?" I question.

"Art thou guilty or nay?" an older gentleman to the left, who looks particularly unpleasant, snaps.

I shake my head. "Nay!"

"So you are denying that you are indeed not a witch? Thou did not afflict a total of three young girls? That you have not been poisoning the town of Salem through various tonics and tinctures?"

Three? I thought it was just Abigail and Betty that accused me of so? There are more? What for? What have I done to deserve such?

"Nay!" I say with a shake of my head. "I am not what you speak. I have never afflicted nor poisoned a soul in my life."

"LIAR!" Reverend Parris hisses from behind me.

I turn to look at him, only to find Reverend Noyes attempting to settle him, though he does so while delivering me a chilling glare in return.

"Let her spew her lies, shall deliver her a sooner hanging," Hathorne says with a shrug.

"So be it," the Chief Justice speaks.

For the next several hours, I am asked countless questions, all of which I answer truthfully to. I do not have a love for the Devil. I do not work for him. I love God, and I have never hurt another. All answers they do not believe and grow angrier with each word.

Finally, they decide to end the trial for the day, rescheduling me to return at a later date, as they must move to the next, I suppose. Turning to move out of the courthouse, my eyes meet Thomas's, and he does not look away this time. I do. He is not who I thought he was, not the man he claims to be. He is weak, craven, and I do not wish to waste another minute upon him.

After being led to the horses, Hutchinson mounts his and begins to walk with me as another man on his horse comes riding alongside us.

"Good day, gentlemen. I was sent to journey towards Ipswich and fetch Osborne for questioning," Thomas says.

"We have more than enough capability, Putnam," Lewis scoffs.

"I have no doubt of that, but I shall follow all the same," he says before looking down at me.

"Good, get up onto the horse."

"Her feet work just as well," Hutchinson argues.

Thomas narrows his eyes at him as he speaks.

"Do we share an issue, Joseph? Is it time already for myself to collect upon the loan I had lent you?"

He squirms in the seat of his saddle as he looks at Thomas, shaking his head.

"No. My apologies. Do with the witch as you please," he says, tossing the chain to Thomas.

He winds it into his arms before extending a free one to me. I stare as if 'tis a snake ready to attack. His patience thins as he rolls his eyes and snaps.

"Now!"

I startle at the harshness of his words before mounting the horse and swinging my leg over. It takes some balance and adjustment before I am seated in front of Thomas due to my growing belly. He doesn't waste a moment to move his mouth close to my ear, whispering words only meant for us two as the others continue on their way.

"I'm so sorry."

I do not acknowledge his words, instead focusing on the road before me.

"Sarah, please," he whispers again.

Still, I do not turn.

"I understand you are angry with me. I am angry with myself. I...have no excuses. I only wish this to be over and everything to go back as it was."

"Before you knew the truth?" I spit towards him.

He furrows his brows. "I thought you have spoken you are not a witch."

"I am not. Not by your definition, or any other. Though if you want to depict me as such, then I may as well be in your eyes."

"Sarah," he whispers pleadingly. "I'm frightened for you, the both of you," he says, reaching around to touch my belly.

"We will face whatever the court decides, without you by my side. You made sure of that."

He's quiet for several moments before he continues.

"The town is in full hysteria. Dozens of people are being accused by the minute. The court appointed cannot keep up. I fear they will begin hangings soon."

"And that bothers you so?" I sneer.

He forces my face to look upon his, Thomas's hand gripping my cheeks with tight force.

"Watching you hang at the end of a rope plagues my nightmares. I'd rather hang myself than witness such a sight."

Fear runs through me at his words, mainly because I know them to be true. I am not a dull woman. I know the court would never rule me innocent, no matter how hard I plead, no matter what evidence I provide. Their minds are decided. I am living on borrowed time. I'll be damned if I allow them to win, allow them to take my life for their evil plot.

Before I fully know what I am doing, I grip the knife Thomas often keeps at his side as I jump off the horse. I am able to steady myself with my hands before running through the meadow to the left. I hear Thomas call for me as the others begin shooting their guns. Still, I run. I run until I come upon a cliff, nowhere to go but down.

"Sarah!" Thomas shouts as he comes running through the bushes, Hutchinson and Lewis on his tail, both weapons drawn.

"Get down!" Lewis shouts.

I turn to face them as I take a step back and then another until my heels feel the ground come to an end.

"Whoa, whoa, whoa!" Thomas shouts, holding out a hand as if that will stop me.

"Come no closer!" I shout as I lift the knife to my throat.

"Do as she says," Thomas snarls.

Surprisingly, Hutchinson and Lewis do as he such as they watch me.

"What are you doing?" Thomas asks, holding out his hands as if he means no harm.

I do not realize I am crying until I taste the salty taste of my tears.

"The outcome shall be the same, at least this way I shall be a master of my own fate. I will not fall prey to the sick games of these trials."

"You know not the outcome of your trial, nor the others. Do not make haste decisions for which you can not undo," Thomas says, taking another step and another towards me.

"Whether my blood be spilled on this cliff or my neck snapped at Gallows Hill, it shall make no difference. Everyone wishes for my death; they wish to bask in it. I shall not give them such satisfaction," I say as I dig the knife into my neck deeper.

"Please, please," Thomas says softly, slowly coming closer. "Think of Dorothy, think of the child that grows in your belly by the day. You want them to live, do you not?"

"Live only for their mother to die?" I ask with a menacing laugh.

"Do not make assumptions. The innocent shall not be slain. If you are as you speak, everything shall be right, shall it not?"

"Aye, let her be, Putnam. If she wants to rid herself, saves us rope!" Hutchinson snarls.

"Silence!" he snaps, turning to face the men for half a second before softening his face to me once more.

"Please, the father of your unborn would never recover from the loss of you two, I can assure it."

I laugh bitterly at his choice of words, so careful not to allow his true affections show.

"Trust in me, the father does not care for either of us. He has made that known."

I close my eyes, shaking my head up to the sky as I ready myself to slit my throat when I feel my arm snatched away from my neck.

Thomas grapples for the knife before twisting my arm in an unnatural way. A scream rips from my chest as my hand releases the knife. It thunks to the ground hollowly as I begin to weep. Despite our audience, Thomas whispers reassurances into my ear as his hand rubs my back soothingly.

"It will be alright. Allow me to help you onto the horse. Let us get you back to Dorothy, yes?"

I sniff and nod, another cry escaping me as Thomas lifts me into his arms and carries me back to the horses.

"Should have let her rid herself," Hutchinson says as Lewis nods his agreement.

Thomas ignores them, setting me upon the horse before climbing up himself. From there, we ride the rest of the way in silence. My tears have long dried, but the pain inside me never fades. Not when we arrive, nor when Thomas's hand leaves mine, and certainly not when he gives me one last look of longing before shutting the iron barred door, leaving the jail with Sarah Osborne in his custody.

Chapter Twelve

Thomas

June 10th 1692

The guilt I faced leaving Sarah in that jail cell yet again has waned with the days that have passed. I have found that if I do not visit, I do not think of her often. I know what type of man that makes me to be, but so be it. There are bigger issues afoot than just my affections. Salem has been plagued with witchcraft. Far worse than we ever imagined. Reverend Noyes has been key in sorting out the sinners from the innocent. Some have been acquitted, but most are guilty, and rightfully so.

My daughter Ann has been afflicted by many since speaking out, and many other girls are facing the same fate at the hands of vengeful witches in hiding. At first, I believed this to be a game that Abigail and Betty had invented to pass the days. I do not *believe Ann would play along in such matters, and I shall not allow it to escalate to my other kin. The fear, the terror, the evil among us. 'Tis real, 'tis dangerous, and it threatens to destroy us all.*

Bridgette Bishop has been accused of afflicting my Ann, and today she faces judgment for such actions. She is the first to be sentenced, the first of many I foresee. God is ever present among us on this holy day, as we extinguish the flames of evil, one witch at a time.

Looking up from my journal, I tuck it away and look to the rope dangling from the tree where George Corwin wraps the end around her neck. The woman sobs in anguish as he does so, while Walcott keeps the horse beneath her steady.

"Bishop, what say you? You stand here charged with sundry acts of witchcraft committed upon the bodies of Ann Putnam, Mercy Lewis, and others," Hathorne says.

"I am innocent. I know nothing of it! I have performed no witchcraft...I am as innocent as the child unborn!" she protests.

I shake my head as Parris scoffs beside me. Not a soul in the crowd believes her lies as Hathorne nods to George. He takes a step back as Walcott does the same before Corwin's hand slaps the behind of his horse, sending it running and her falling. Her neck breaks with a loud snap that causes gasps to echo through the crowd. Griggs approaches the dangling body, searching for a pulse before officially pronouncing her dead.

Women and children hide their faces as some of the weaker men turn green. Not me. Instead of sorrow or sadness at a life lost, I feel relief, pleasure even. 'Twas not an innocent life lost today, but a demonic one. One that we should all be glad to be rid of. I pray for more reveals, more executions. Death to all witches, I say.

My words have trouble matching my insides, though. I can feel all of this, believe every word of what the court says, and still feel doubt when it comes to my Sar...Mrs. Good. A small piece of me hopes she is acquitted, though I know any hope at our future is all but burnt to ashes, I still think of her often. Think of our growing child. Though I do my best to banish such thoughts as they pain me so.

I am doing right by my village, my family. I must put all before myself. No matter how much I desire the opposite.

Chapter Thirteen

Sarah

I have gone back and forth to Salem Village many times since my first day in trial. Each time, I refuse to allow them to hear what they desire. I'm so thankful 'tis that way too. In the beginning, Thomas urged me to comply, to accept the charges of witchcraft and hope they will spare me. I know that not to be true, though. Bridgette Bishop has been hung, a kind older woman who has never looked wrong at another. If she had little hope, then what fate may lie with me?

Dorothy has begun to lose weight despite the rations I provide her. 'Tis not enough. My little girl's light is dimming, and I am unable to help it. Though selfishly, I am joyous to be with her, I fear for what fate shall meet her. At first, she did not know why she was brought here. Then she was brought to trial, where she later explained Ann Putnam had accused her of witchcraft. I do not know why it hurt so much to hear that. Ann is a mirror image of her mother, in looks and actions. I have no doubt twas her mother who planted the very idea. Still, I cannot banish the thought that if Thomas wanted to, he could have intervened. He promised to love and care for Dorothy as his own, and this is the treatment she receives? That I?

He has not been back since delivering me from my trial. In these months, it has allowed me time to think and finally see with open eyes. His words were a farce, his intentions hollow. He desired a distraction, a mistress, and I so foolishly became that for him. I was desperate for freedom, for love, I fell for his tricks, and now here I rot, his child growing inside me, and my own dying daughter in result.

My discomfort grows with the day, and if this baby grows the same way as Dorothy did, I expect the birth within a few fortnights. I know not what to think of that. 'Tis one thing to live with his child inside me, but to look upon its face? I am unsure what feelings will arrive. Will it be joy? For the gift of God is truly something to be celebrated. Or will I feel anger? Pain? Sorrow? I wish to hold the baby inside for as long as I am able, because I have no desire to find out.

A sickly sounding cough rasps through the cell, and I look over to see Elizabeth Booth curled into herself. She is shaking as if she is cold and moaning in pain. Checking to ensure Dorothy is asleep, I slip beside her, feeling her head with the back of my hand. 'Tis the fever indeed. The conditions in here are less than poor, and many are beginning to pass away from such. Sarah Osborne died a quick yet painful death of the very same, I gathered. Though I hope God shall not judge me too harshly, for I made no effort to heal her. Still, from what I can tell, I would imagine Elizabeth does not have long.

Reaching for the bowl of murky water, I place it into the sliver of moonlight pouring in from the slatted window high above us. 'Tis a full moon tonight, which means if I have any chance of achieving success, tonight is the night to do so.

Letting the bowl sit in the light, I close my eyes as I imagine her healing, imagine the sickness inside her being pulled out from the power of the light. I continue these images for several hours, until I grow tired and unfocused. Then, I lift the bowl to her mouth.

"Drink, drink," I whisper in encouragement.

Elizabeth blinks up at me, her sweat dotted face looking more sickly by the moment as she parts her lips and takes small sips. I nod at her to continue, and she does as I ask before I pull the bowl away from her.

I rub my hand gently upon her back, and she smiles at me weakly before returning to her position. All I can hope is that I was successful.

"Y-you really are a w-witch, aren't you?" Roger Toothaker shakes from the corner.

He, too, looks to be sick with the fever.

"No, but I know remedies to help those who need it," I say as I lift the water, gesturing to him.

He snarls at me as if I have offended him. Surely the physician he is thinks nothing of my methods.

"Keep away from me! I want nothing to do with whatever you concocted over there. You are no healer. You gave her but water you muttered over."

I do not argue with him, for I have not the energy. So, I place the bowl down and return to Dorothy's sleeping side.

My eyes do not miss the way Roger stares at the bowl longingly as a coughing fit takes over. The stubbornness inside of him does not allow him to move, though. It bothers me none as I close my eyes, continuing to visualize. This time, 'tis not for Elizabeth's health, but mine and Dorothy's freedom.

Chapter Fourteen

Thomas

June 29th 1692

My palms have been sweating, my hand trembling for weeks in anticipation for this day. 'Tis one I knew was coming, yet prayed it would be held off. I have overseen many trials, many accusations, and hangings. Though this is the one I have long feared, for I ought not know how to feel of such.

Today is the final trial for Sarah Good, as well as others. Though she is the only one I care for. I have instructed the jailer to keep me informed on her condition. He wrote to me Monday of last week, speaking of how her pregnancy has advanced. She can often not stand on her own and requires aid. Elizabeth Booth has been an ally to her since recovering from a sickness and has looked after young Dorothy as well. That brings me peace, along with guilt, for it should be me taking care over those girls. I would like to speak on why I am not, I just...my mind is not well. These thoughts and truths all blend together, leaving me unsure of where to go or what to do. The only thing I can think to do is stay the course, seek out evil, and deliver peace. 'Tis the notion that allows me sleep at night, at least.

My writing is sloppy upon this horse, but it helps to release my thoughts onto parchment. As if I am allowing them to be set free. When I arrive at the jail in Ipswich, unease fills me as myself and several others dismount and journey towards the entrance.

One by one, names are called out as we collect our charges. Sarah is the last, and she looks to Dorothy with tear filled eyes, promising her all will be well. A promise I made and broke not too long ago.

I keep my emotions steady as I allow her to walk first out the door. My eyes cannot help but take in the way she walks, the weight of her child too much to bear on her thin frame. *Our* child.

Memories of impassioned nights beside the creek flash behind my eyes as I do. What a different time that feels like. A time of excitement and joy, peace, love...if I could do anything, turn back time, I'd go back to nights like those. I'd have taken Sarah into my arms, and we'd have run as planned. Never to look back. A fantastical plan like that has no promise now. Everything has changed, I have changed, I have no doubt she has as well. We are not those people anymore, and though I know that is my blame to bear, there is no undoing it.

The accused begin walking on foot, chains in hands of the men here for them, but I will not allow Sarah to walk. Helping her upon the horse, I rest my hand onto her belly before it moves. I startle as our eyes meet, and I keep my hand in place. Again, a kick, hard enough to practically feel a whole foot through her. A tear falls down her face, matching a deep sadness inside of me.

My hand rubs against her belly, as if a way to soothe it in such. Soon, the baby settles, and Sarah pulls herself upon the horse. We ride in silence for quite some time until I speak lowly for only our ears to listen.

"When will you give birth?"

For a moment, I do not think she will grant me a response. I should see no reason why I deserve one, and am accepting of such, until her sweet voice rings out into my ear.

"I imagine soon. The baby feels as if it has flipped, and I have begun feeling the practice pains."

I nod at that, swallowing roughly as I ask the thing on my mind I ought not speak.

"I would like to be there, for the birth. To hold your hand, hold the baby. If you will allow it."

She turns to look at me, indignation in her features.

"Whatever for?"

I open my mouth to speak, though I do not have a word that comes to mind. She turns away to face forward once more as she speaks.

"You are Thomas Putnam. I have never heard you ask permission for anything in your life."

She is not wrong.

"'Tis the least I can do, to grant you this privacy if you so desire."

"Well, I do. I so desire as much privacy away from you as possible. I beg of you, allow any other to escort me from here on out. The sight of you sours my stomach," she sneers.

Her words punch holes into my chest, though I stay silent, allowing it to do so. 'Tis less than I deserve for how I have betrayed her. But she often forgets how she betrayed me. I loved her so, and she deceived me. She claims to be a woman of light, but I see no way. Not for what she has admitted to me in private. She is...a woman I could never be with...never have. And I hate her for it.

The tension inside me rises with each step of my horse's hooves, and when we arrive in town, I feel as if I will be sick. One by one, we dismount from the horses, escorting our charges inside the courthouse. 'Tis a full crowd this day, my entire family there to bear witness. My wife wears a smug grin, casting cruel eyes to Sarah in a way that fills me with rage.

Hutchinson speaks first, calling all attention forward.

"We have come together for the final sentencing of Rebecca Nurse, Susannah Martin, Sarah Wildes, Elizabeth Howe, and Sarah Good. The findings are as follows. In the case of Rebecca Nurse, guilty. Susannah Martin, guilty. Sarah Wildes, guilty. Elizabeth Howe, guilty."

I know the next words that are about to leave his mouth, yet I am unable to face them. I close my eyes and tense, as if a physical blow is coming.

"Sarah Good, guilty."

Just like that. 'Tis as if a gun shot has exploded inside of my chest. In one way and out the other, I am hollow. The other women cry out and sob, but not Sarah. She remains composed, frozen like a statue.

"All five have been found of witchcraft and are due to hang at Gallows Hill immediately."

"No!" I shout before I can help it.

The entire courtroom stills as all eyes land upon me. I meet Parris and Noyes, their eyes narrowed in curiosity as I continue.

"Chief Justice, Mrs. Good is with child. Surely the child ought not suffer the sins of the mother?"

Even as I speak the words, they taste of ash on my tongue.

He nods his head from side to side as if he were weighing his options before nodding.

"Agreed, we shall not forsake the unborn for the living's sins. Hang date shall be set once the child has been birthed. Ensure Ipswich is aware of the communication necessary."

I nod my agreement and settle an idea in my mind then and there.

I may not be able to have Sarah the way my soul craves, but I can have our baby. I can love them and cherish them and raise them in her absence. Then one day, when they are old enough, I will teach them about their mother, only the best parts.

I cannot save her, but I will save my child.

Chapter Fifteen

Sarah

I 'm lying on the cold, hard floor, the midnight sky granting little light into the cell as I stroke Dorothy's hair while she sleeps. Death is coming, quicker than I'd ever imagined. I can feel it in my bones, in the air, and I know there is no escaping it.

I fear what will happen to Dorothy when I go. Will she suffer the same fate? Will she be released and turned over to William to serve a lifetime beneath his fist? What other option will be left?

I fear for my unborn child, who is due any day now. What little time I have with them will be spent in a prison cell, and when I am gone, they will not know a thing about me. I expect Thomas will not acknowledge either of my children, which means they will have nothing. No one. The guilt of knowing such things gnaws inside my belly like a starved animal.

A pain rips through me, dull at first before becoming sharper. I wince as it occurs again and again. Oh God. It's happening.

I squirm in place as I move so as not to wake Dorothy. My stirring alerts Elizabeth Booth, though, as I attempt to hold in my cries before letting them out with a sputter.

"Sarah? What is the matter?" she asks.

I hold my belly tightly as I look to her, another contraction ripping through me.

"It is time," I say through a pained moan.

"For truth?" she asks.

I nod my head as a cry escapes me. Elizabeth jumps to her feet.

"Guard! Guard! Help!"

As slowly as he is able, an older jailer comes up to the cell, sneering at Elizabeth as he speaks.

"What is the ruckus for?"

"Sarah is enduring childbirth! The baby is coming. We need a doctor," she begs.

"We do not have one. Since Toothaker croaked, we have yet to have one around these parts."

"Then fetch one if you must!" she snaps. "Or at the least provide me with towels and warm water."

The young jailer who treats me well, thanks to Thomas, comes over, his hair a mess as if he has just awoken from his sleep, as he takes in the scene.

"Is she having the baby?" he asks.

"Appears so." The other jailer shrugs.

As if a bucket of water has been dumped upon his head, the sleep leaves the young jailer's eyes as he takes off in a run.

"Where art thou off to?" the older jailer shouts.

"To notify Putnam!"

"What business does he have?" he calls back but does not earn a response before the guard is through the doors and outside.

"Oh nooooo!" I moan as another painful contraction rips through me.

"Water and towels, make haste!" Elizabeth snaps once more before facing me. "'Tis okay, Sarah. I will assist you."

I wince as I shake my head.

"I am not your burden to bear."

"Nonsense," she says, effectively hushing me. "Get onto your hands and knees, that will allow the baby to come easier. Stand if you are able."

I shake my head, unable to speak, let alone stand. Something is wrong. Labor did not feel such a way when I had my Dorothy. Perhaps it's that I'm so very hungry, so very thirsty, that my body has been aching and in pain for months now. I know not the source, only that I can hardly stand it.

Another sharp pain rips through my body that has me howling like an animal. I feel Elizabeth rub soothing circles against my back, but her touch provides no comfort as my body breaks out into cold sweats.

When the pain eases momentarily, she praises me, brushing my hair away from my sweat dotted forehead. She looks to another beside us as she speaks.

"Begin counting! Now!"

I hear the sounds of someone counting the seconds that pass and allow myself to drift in a delirious haze before the next pain comes.

"Two minutes apart. Your baby is coming soon. You can do this, Sarah."

I shake my head and whimper. Why is labor quickening so? It felt like hours, days even, last time. Something is wrong. This is all wrong.

I do my best to stay upon my hands and knees, but a wave of pain knocks me down, curling into myself as the old jailor brings a single towel and a small cup of water.

Elizabeth looks to him in shock as he sets the items down and walks away. She scoffs, muttering beneath her breath as she dips her hands into the warm water, washing them before feeling between my legs.

"Okay, I see the baby's head, Sarah. Ready...push!"

I do as she says, gritting my teeth as I push.

"Good job, Mama!" Dorothy says in a way that makes me smile.

I look at her tiredly as Elizabeth speaks once more.

"Again."

Taking a deep breath, I push with everything inside of me, relief filling me as I feel the baby leave my body as a cry fills the jail. Euphoria overtakes me as I laugh, Elizabeth handing the baby to me before resting it upon my chest. Elizabeth continues tending to me as I focus on my sweet baby girl.

"Mercy," I whisper as I look upon her. "My little Mercy."

"I like that name, Mama," Dorothy says as she reaches out, touching the baby gently with an awe inspired smile that rivals my own.

"Me too," I say as I look to Elizabeth.

She nods and smiles at me. "You did well, and the placenta followed her easily. Much joy to you all."

"Many thanks, Elizabeth," I say, holding my hand out for hers.

She smiles, taking my hand and squeezing it. Mercy begins to fuss in my arms, but I do not mind, for this moment is perfect.

I fell asleep, and the blame rests solely upon me. I rested Mercy beneath my dress to provide her as much protection from the cold as I was able, but it wasn't enough. When I woke from my rest, I pressed my lips to her forehead and found her cold and stiff. Her pale pink lips had turned blue, and her soft body was now unmoving. With the help of Elizabeth, we tried to revive her, but she had already been gone for too long. I haven't it in me to put her down, though. I fear if I do, I'll never be able to breathe once more.

The jail door is suddenly thrown open, two pairs of footsteps rushing down the hall before stopping upon us. The early morning sun is beginning to peek out and welcome the new day. A joyous start, though nothing in the world feels joyous anymore.

A frantic Thomas fills my vision as the young jailer opens the gate.

"Did I miss the birth?" he asks as he rushes to me.

I stare up at him, not able to feel a thing as a tear falls from my eyes.

"Yes."

"Where is the baby?" he asks, his head moving around before he takes a closer look at my arms. A smile fills his face for a moment before understanding comes to follow.

"Why does it not move?"

Guilt, anger, rage, heartache. They all swirl inside me as I attempt to comprehend how to speak of what has happened, what has occurred because of the conditions we are in. Because I was forced here. Because of him.

"Dead," I grit through clenched teeth, shaking as I do.

Horror strikes his face as he looks upon her and me, shaking his head in disbelief. He stands to his feet as he begins pacing the cell, digging his fingers through his hair as he mumbles to himself.

"No, no, no, no! 'Tis not how it should have been! Was it born as so?"

"No," Elizabeth says from the corner. "She appeared fine. We fell asleep, and she...did not wake."

"She?" Thomas asks, tears filling his eyes as he looks upon me.

"Twas a girl. Mercy," I say, as the pain in my chest slowly eases, only leaving room for resentment and rage.

"Mercy," he whispers beneath his breath, shaking his head in reverence.

Carefully, he bends down beside me to take a closer look. When he does, his fingertips graze against her cold skin before a pained cry escapes him. His sobs are rough and without care for the audience that grows among us. Something about his cries loosens something inside of me as I feel more tears roll down my cheek.

Thomas attempts to wrap his arms around me, but I do not

allow it, for why should I comfort him when he turned his back upon us? Had it not been for his betrayal, she would not have been born in such conditions. We could have had a doctor, a warm bed. She could have lived. Her death hangs upon his head, as it does on my own. He will not receive a bit of comfort from me for the rest of my days, however few there may be.

Thomas looks upon me in shock at my refusal before he appears to think the same thoughts as I. The guilt is written across his face, and he does his best to tuck away his emotions, straightening his appearance before standing to leave.

He does not offer me another word, nor do I to him. The man has taken more than any should, broken more than any could. He has been the deliverer of my greatest joy, and the executer of my Damnation.

Chapter Sixteen

Thomas

July 19th 1692

My heart is filled with so much sorrow. Sorrow I didn't know I was capable of experiencing. The ache in my chest has not dulled since that morning. The jailer of Ipswich arrived at my door in the middle of the night in a panic. I answered with irritation, but the moment I looked upon his face, I knew what was happening.

The entire ride there, I pushed my horse as fast as it could go. I was racing time, I knew that much. I did not know I was racing a chance to witness my child alive.

Her pale blue face is burned in my mind, forever embedded, forever a part of me. The hollow, gaunt look of Sarah as she spoke of it was spine chilling. Not for her lack of emotion, though 'tis what you might *assume. No, I saw the pain in her beautiful eyes. The heartache I felt in my own chest. She was numb, in shock, and truthfully, I believe I am the same.*

I insisted on taking the baby home to Salem for a proper burial. I could not put faith in the jailers at Ipswich to take the care Mercy deserved. Surprisingly, Sarah did not fight me. She looked to me with such hatred that it turned my stomach as I took our lifeless child from her arms before tucking her against me.

I buried her beneath the tree where Sarah and I spent our nights together. It felt right to have her laid to rest in the place where her mother and father were at their happiest. Where we dreamed of the life we would give her, the one we would live together.

A sharp knock comes from my door. I shake my thoughts away, tucking my journal safely inside my pocket as I look to see my visitor. When the door is opened, Edward is standing there, dressed in black, as he looks to me.

"Art thou ready?"

Ready? As if he could ever possibly understand that I shall never be ready for this day. This moment. I had no idea how I would manage to get out of bed this morning, let alone be ready. I am, though. As ready as I am able. My clothes are put on with pride, I'm freshly bathed, and together, we set off for Gallows Hill.

Edward does not speak, and I am grateful for as much. He knows of my relations with Sarah, knows that it was my child in her belly. He knows nothing, though. He knows not of my care for her, the love. He knows not of the torment I have suffered, pulled between the woman who holds my heart and my dedication to the Church and townsfolk of Salem. If I was not a better man, I would have run away with Sarah, started our new life just as promised. As a Puritan man, I have a responsibility. No matter the love I feel, I shall not give into the Devil's whispers. For I know, despite her words, he is the one who holds her heart. Who holds all of those practicing witchcraft, and for that, there is only one path.

Sheriff Corwin is readying the nooses and the stools for the sentenced to stand upon before their execution. Nearly the entire town is present this morning. Today is not just any hanging. Today, a total of five witches shall be hanged for their wrongdoings and evil work. Including my Sarah.

I attempt to persuade myself to listen to reason and think truly. Sarah is a witch; she has denied it by title, but not by practice. She spins tales with pretty words of being a lover of God but harnesses powers gifted from Satan himself. This be the only answer that should bring God glory and justice.

A fairytale of good witches is just that, a fairytale, and though it pains me, I do not believe her.

Since the first few arrests, the town's eyes have been opened. More witches than we ever believed to be possible reside with us. Salem is not safe. We must purge the land of the unholy occupants before God almighty strikes us down himself, for I fear we are facing to be the next Sodom and Gomorrah if we do not take action.

For a moment, I consider standing in the back. Perhaps if I do not set eyes on her, the ache inside me will fade. Though even I know 'tis too cowardly of an act to perform. Slowly, Edward and I move through the crowd till we are but at the front. Five nooses hang upon a structure built by several men in town. One of whom to be William Good, the abusive bastard that I have yet to see at his own wife's hanging.

I sneer to myself, shaking my head as Parris approaches my side.

"What a joyous day it is this morning," he says to me with a nod.

"'Tis indeed," I say, only bearing little lie.

'Tis a good day. We are closer to cleansing our village, protecting our children, winning the favor of God's love once more. I just wish this damned ache inside me would fade soon.

Several others join us at the front, the most dedicated of the townsfolk. Walcott, Preston, Griggs, and more. They all share the desire for protection Parris and I feel, the need to purge the land of evil and be a town of good folk and value once more.

They are a good lot, better than the conspirators I have heard whisperings of. Some think the trials are moving too quickly, that the process is not done thoroughly. They have the arrogance to call us hasty in our accusations and sentencing. I say anyone who thinks or speaks so must be a witch in blood or heart, for they ought not spread lies for any other reason.

My eyes move around the crowd, resting on those I know to be suspicious. We will seek them out, one by one, and we shall see for real and for truth who stands with us...or with them.

My attention is elsewhere when the convicted are led to the Gallows. The crowd begins to erupt, booing, screaming, and even cursing towards them. Four of the women hide their faces in shame, rightfully so. One, though, does not. Instead, she meets the eyes of every last person in the crowd, as if committing them to memory. Though I desire to drop my eyes before her gaze reaches my own, I refuse.

When those beautiful eyes land upon me, my stomach flips, though I am unsure if it is from disgust or desire. Perhaps a mixture of the two. Disappointment fills her features as she sneers at me before approaching the stool before her. All others have the nooses already around their necks, quiet sobs echoing through the trees as Sarah shakes her head and begins to run.

Ingersoll and Corwin fight with her before securing the noose around her neck. She continues fighting and struggling as Corwin lifts her upon her stool, holding her in place as Reverend Noyes addresses her first.

"Sarah Good! Thou hast been proven to be a witch, there be no denying it. Admit to your sins to save your immortal soul or suffer with the damned!"

Everyone listens with bated breath when Sarah finishes fighting, her body stilling in a moment. She closes her eyes calmly, breathing in and out before what looks like fire burns beneath her eyes.

"You're a liar! I'm no more a witch than you are a wizard!"

Gasps of outrage and horror echo through the crowd as Noyes's face turns red with fury.

"If you take my life away, God will give you blood to drink!"

Noyes's anger grows as he closes the distance between them as Sarah looks to me. All of the anger and outrage is still heavy upon her face, though the fire in her eyes has dimmed, drenched with immense sadness. Her mouth moves, though no sound escapes. I'm able to make out the beginning of it, though.

I hate...

The next moment, Noyes kicks the stool beneath her feet, and the sound of her neck snapping echoes in the air around us. I audibly gasp, though I was prepared for it. My body jolts as I see the woman I once thought I loved hanging by her neck, swinging in the breeze.

Still. Lifeless. Gone.

My eyes are still upon hers when I hear the sound of another stool being kicked, followed by another snap of a neck. Sarah's face swings to face me once more, and I burn the sight into my mind before closing my eyes and turning away.

Without a word, I begin pushing through the crowd, moving to go anywhere but here. I hear several call out for me, but I ignore each as I move on. I allow the sight of Sarah's hanging to be forever placed in my memories, right beside my sweet Mercy. I take every bit of the hurt I feel inside me and allow it to consume me. Anger. Pain. Fear. Rage. It all flows through my veins as I open my eyes, feeling more powerful than I have for all of my life.

After all, name a man who is more powerful than a man with nothing to lose.

Epilogue

Thomas

May 1st 1693

This sinful day, we have been delivered grave news. Governor Phips has ordered that the court of Oyer and Terminer be disbanded or treason shall be faced. We have tried to seek reason with the man, but he will have no part of it. No doubt he has been coerced or corrupt. Perhaps both. He does not know a thing, living his lavish lie in Boston. He does not know the evil we have overcome, the horrors we have faced.

Nineteen have met their just fate, and hundreds more are to follow. Though with the Governor's order, I foresee the lot of them being set free within a fortnight or two. Even Dorothy.

That simply will not do.

Setting my journal down, I look around Ingersoll's tavern, where I have asked those truly loyal to gather. That list has grown quite short as most have begged off or even slandered the name of what we are achieving here in Salem. Better without them all, I say.

The very idea of witches we know to be true being allowed to live? When Sarah was not gifted such? No, 'tis all or nothing, and since we have begun, we must finish this. With or without the Governor's approval.

"What hast thou gathered us for?" Hutchinson calls out.

Standing to my feet, I tuck my journal into my coat pocket as I begin pacing the room.

"Brothers, lend me your ear. We are at war. We are at war with a great and vile enemy. One that plots to destroy the very fabric of our lives. They are hungry for our town, our virtue, our souls, and we cannot allow it!"

Every man is solely focused on me, a feeling I have grown more accustomed to as I have taken over a lead position during these trials. 'Tis a feeling unmatched by any.

"The Governor wishes us to abandon our beliefs, allow evil to run rampant among us, but I simply cannot, and I know you are all in agreement."

Several heads nod in the tavern as I continue.

"Though the court has been disbanded, and our trials may be halted, I urge you all to hear me now. We cannot allow our work to stop; we cannot allow our guards to fall. We do not need a court or trials or the Governor's damned permission for a thing!" I snarl.

"What does thou mean?" Walcott asks.

"A brotherhood," I continue. "A brotherhood to watch over each other, over our town. A brotherhood that is thicker than blood or water. One that once entered into, cannot be broken nor weakened. In numbers, we find strength; in brotherhood, we find protection."

"And what will our brotherhood be doing, Putnam?" Parris asks, ever morally just.

"Nothing God would not ask of us, Samuel," I answer before addressing the crowd once more.

"Salem needs us, dare I say Massachusetts needs us. This is not just an agreement, not just a promise to remain a faithful servant to God. This is a promise to remain a faithful servant to each other, to the brotherhood, to our safety."

To my surprise, a few uneasy looks pass upon faces, and I waste not a moment in calling such out.

"Why do you look to me in such a way, Ingersoll?"

He appears spooked as he looks around the room before shaking his head.

"I am unable to understand why we need to promise so much. Does it not feel as if we are taking another religion?"

"Blasphemy!" I scoff. "This be not a religion, but a community...a society operated in secret. One that will protect the town of Salem, that will seek out evil and deliver justice in God's name. Tell me this, do you think the Nurse family will not come for us? For we all know, they harbor hate towards us all. And the Carys? Ushers? Aldens? What of those who escaped before and during the arrests? Every man, woman, and child is a threat until we deem otherwise. Just because the Governor dubs the trials over, does not make it so. If we allow them to strike first, it shall be our necks snapped at Gallows Hill, mark every word I speak."

Understanding begins to fill the room as several heads nod. To my surprise, the first to rise to his feet in support is Parris. I thought the goody reverend would struggle with such a premise.

He extends his hand for my own, shaking it as he speaks.

"I shall follow you anywhere you lead."

"As will I," Edward says as he too stands.

"And I," Griggs agrees.

Preston and Hutchinson look to each other before standing.

Then, one by one, Ingersoll, Walcott, Lewis, and finally Stroughton all rise to their feet. My eyes meet each, silently thanking them for their commitment. Together, we have some of the strongest families of Salem. Together, we have the most impassioned members of our community. With their support, we will create a group that not only protects, but thrives, far from the government's reach. We shall be an operation of our own support. A society. A brotherhood.

The Brethren.

Extended Epilogue

Thomas Putnam III

July 25th, 1699

'Tis my eighteenth birthday on this summer evening, though it feels as if it is a day not worth celebrating. The wake of my father's death has rocked the very core of Salem. Though nearly two months have passed, life has not quite moved past his legacy. My mother is distraught and unwell, my siblings are filled with a mixture of emotions, but it is the town who suffers the most. He was not just a wealthy influence, he was a leader, a guide, a savior.

The trials may have ended seven years ago, but his work was far from over. With the end of the trials came the birth of something greater, something holier, something everlasting.

The Brethren has been built brick by brick at the hands of my father and the others who have dubbed themselves the Elders. Each family has taken up position inside the town's hierarchy, far more encompassing than just businessmen and landowners. They are investigators, protectors, and executioners.

My father did not allow me knowledge of Brethren business until three years ago. As they were constructing Gallows Hill University, he sat me and my brothers down to explain the work he has created. The university took years to construct, a massive structure that no other town in the New World has been blessed with yet. Not only is the building of impressive nature, designed to train and groom only the best of future generations, but the significance of the land is pertinent. Built upon the graves of those tried, the university stands proudly upon Gallows Hill, forever a reminder of the sacrifice and determination the Elders have made and continue to make to protect us from our enemies.

My attendance at Gallows Hill commences with the coming of fall, but as the heir of my father's title and position inside the Brethren, my work has just begun. True to his suspicions and concerns, a force has been created. Escapees, descendants of those tried, and some we never even suspected, have rallied together. They call themselves the Coven. As if that wasn't the clearest proof of the evil they embody.

They seek revenge for the justice that has been served. They are in search of revenge. If only they weren't half as intelligent as us with a quarter of our numbers. We are stronger, smarter, and larger than they shall ever be, and we are growing by the day. I have sent letters to influential families we are close with in Boston as well as New York, inviting them to join our society. My father wished to keep the Brethren private, to only include the Elder families, but I say to hell with that. Strength is in numbers, and power is in the size of your influence. Besides, he is now unable to make decisions as he rots in the earth with those who have fallen before him.

A new order is rising from what he has built, and with my direction, we shall transform the Brethren into a society greater than any monarchy, any society that has ever been. We shall rule with the power of the Egyptians, the strength of the Romans, and protect the values of England herself. Under God and for his name, we shall cleanse this land, and the next, and we shall not stop until every last witch be charred and beneath the dirt.

I twist the ring he hand commissioned for himself and the others around my finger. The curled B stamped upon the precious metal gleams in the glow of the torch lit room as I wait for the others to join. This shall be our first meeting since my father's passing, and only my second that I am witnessing, let alone in control of.

As the others file through the tunnels and into the room, they each take their seats at the table, their heirs standing behind them as I have instructed them to do so. Until tonight, I was the only heir to have been afforded the privilege of attending a meeting. Another change I am seeing to.

"Brothers, welcome. It pains me greatly to be here in place of my father, who was truly a great man."

The words are only half truth. As a man, he was truly great. As a father...he was a swine at best.

"Why hast thou demanded our young be invited?" Walcott snaps.

I turn to him, lifting an eyebrow as I look upon Lenord, my best friend and his son. He takes a step behind his father, clasping his shoulder with a swift grip as he nods.

"So that we shall be well trained and ready for when your time of passing arrives."

His father looks to him, understanding the threat that has been laid upon his feet as my uncle chimes in.

"Why do you assume you should take your father's place, boy? You have no seniority here."

I look upon him with consideration. He has been near manic since I have assumed the throne, and I notice that growing with each day. Something must be done about him, and soon.

Looking to Jeremiah Griggs, I nod my head to him, confirming our previous discussion. My uncle must perish, but 'tis too soon to assert my power with violence. That time will come. I confided that when my uncle is to pass, it must be done with no ties to myself or the Brethren, and he agreed. His outcry was confirmation enough that this matter must be taken care of immediately, and who better than the physician's son? A man knowledgeable in medicines, ailments, and how the body lives...and dies.

"I am the best man for the position. I believe in the cause and will commit my life, my children's lives, and the lives of all my descendants to protect it. 'Tis not just about being vigilant of our protections, we must stay proactive. We must seek the witches out, chase them out of the shadows and into the fire, send them back to the pits of hell for which their souls were birthed from."

Murmurs of agreement echo through the room as I nod. Standing to lead the way, I guide the Elders out of the room and through the tunnel, where a keeper is standing with robes for each. The men look upon them in confusion as I encourage them to take the exquisite material. A merchant was peddling through town, and I placed an order that shall sustain him till winter. His thanks were received by many, and now our society may be clothed properly, in unity.

I slip on my own robe, flipping the hood over my head as I lead the others to the cemetery inside the university, where the fire has been prepared. I have spent many months studying the Coven, taking in their every move. From what I understand, their gatherings around a fire is most sacred to them, so I find much joy in the irony of us emulating such practices.

One by one, each man gathers to complete a circle around the fire as I speak to the group.

"Brothers, the work we shall do is not easy, but necessary. For the good of our families, Salem, and the new world. Lend me your hand in our efforts, and we shall remain ever victorious in the Lord's honor."

"Aye!" Parris cheers enthusiastically, a bloodthirsty look you would not expect upon a reverend. I quite like the sight, though.

Reaching into my inner pocket, I pull out the pages I have torn from my father's journal. For years, I wondered what he was scrawling upon those pages, keeping hidden from all around him. Two weeks with it, and I understood the desire. He was in love. With Sarah Good. With a witch! He consummated such affections and created life. The Good child that died at Ipswich was my kin, his blood. The guilt and disgust ate him alive for years to come, each page a proof to that.

I did not breathe a word to anyone, for doing so could damage my reputation and position. Who would follow in the steps of an heir to a traitor? Not a sane soul alive. I carefully selected which pages to dispose of, but the others will do nicely in telling our history. I shall pass the teachings down of what really happened in Salem all those years ago to my children, and their children, and on and on. All I can wish is that my father's sinful acts and disgraceful choices will burn with these pages.

Throwing them into the fire, a satisfaction rolls through me as I watch the parchment turn to ash, floating into the sky as if God does not wish me to be in their presence for a moment longer. Finally, our time has arrived.

"Maleficis esse mori," I shout.

"Maleficis esse mori," the room echoes.

Death to witches. Death to them all.

Thank You

Thank you so much for stepping back into the past with me! That old English was nothing to mess with! Hopefully this provided a little clarity as to what sparked the ideals and traditions of the Brethren, thus setting everything we know in motion!

If you haven't read the Gallows Hill trilogy, now is the time to start! Dive in now with Deceit and enjoy the ride!

Gallows Hill Series—a dark academia reverse harem
Deceit
Descent
Demise

Standalones
Graves—an MFM stalker romance
Deliverance—an FF secret society romance (spin-off from Gallows Hill)
Gratify—a forbidden age gap
Jagged Harts—an MMA enemies to lovers

The ONS Series—interconnected forbidden romances
One Night Seduction
One Night Scandal - Coming Soon
One Night Surrender - Coming Soon

The Alphaletes Series—interconnected football romances

The Loyalties We Break
The Walls We Break
The Hearts We Break
The Rules We Break

Reviews mean everything to indie authors, so if you could take a moment to leave a review, I would be so thankful!

Review on Amazon & Goodreads

Find me on Instagram, TikTok, Facebook, and my Facebook Reader Group

Make sure you are subscribed to my newsletter and following me on socials to stay up to date on any upcoming releases, special announcements, and giveaways!

Acknowledgments

To my Alpha, Sara, I love you so much! I'm forever thankful for you not only as my PA and Alpha but as my best friend. I treasure you deeply and know without a doubt this story would not have been HALF what it is without you. Shoutout for the therapy scene, that was all thanks to your beautiful brain!

To my Beta's, Arianna, Mackenzie and Rachel, I adore you! Each of you brought something unique and incredibly valuable to this book. I will never be able to thank you all enough for your opinions, perspectives and willingness to help me mold this raw story into something I'm so proud of! Thank you all for your hard work, patience and just being flat out amazing.

To my editors, Brittany and Slasher, literally you two are out here doing the lord's work. No one would even be able to understand my gibberish if it wasn't for you two. Thank you for always helping me create the most clear and proper wording without ever losing my voice. I love you both dearly!

To my street team and ARC readers, thank you all for your support! Every page read, every review left, and every post made truly means the world. I'm not even a little shy to admit that I have hands down the best people behind me.

To my readers, whether this is your first book by me, or you've been by my side since day one, thank you. There are millions of authors out there, billions of books and you chose mine. Each one of you pushes me to write when my fingers ache, plot when my brain is mush and keep moving forward when I'm ready to give up. You all are the best readers anyone could ask for and I love each one of you desperately.

www.ingramcontent.com/pod-product-compliance
Lightning Source LLC
Chambersburg PA
CBHW031544310726
48971CB00008B/2612